Uniform with this volume:

Hugh Hood: *The Collected Stories*

I: Flying a Red Kite

II: A Short Walk in the Rain

Hugh Hood

The Isolation Booth

THE COLLECTED STORIES III

For Barry and Frances
Wainwright
Week of October 20th 1991
From one half of the
Hampton Crescent
arts powerhouse
to the other, with love
Hugh Hood

Loreen Mallory

Grenados!
Goyas!
Angela Cheng!
what else?

The Porcupine's Quill, Incorporated

CANADIAN CATALOGUING IN PUBLICATION DATA

Hood, Hugh.
The isolation booth : the collected stories III

ISBN 0-88984-119-5

I. Title.

PS8515.04917 1991 C813'.54 C91-094216-1
PR9199.3.H6617 1991

Published by The Porcupine's Quill, Inc., 68 Main Street, Erin, Ontario NOB 1TO with financial assistance from The Canada Council and the Ontario Arts Council.

Distributed by The University of Toronto Press, 5201 Dufferin Street, Downsview, Ontario M3H 5T8.

Cover is after a painting by Noreen Mallory.

Readied for the press by Doris Cowan.

Printed and bound by The Porcupine's Quill. The stock is Zephyr laid, and the type, Galliard.

For Howard Roiter,
friend and colleague
of many years,
with affection
and admiration

Contents

Author's Introduction

THESE STORIES were written between March 1957 and October 1966 and are presented here in chronological order. They aren't unpublished stories; each of them achieved magazine publication. The title story was my very first to be published. None of them has been collected in a book until now; they are the very last of my early stories to appear in book form. I have a special affection for them because I remember so clearly the circumstances in which they were written, the original story ideas, the pleasure I took in their magazine appearances and the place the individual pieces took in my long struggle with the form of the short story, an unending struggle.

Sometimes I ask myself why I didn't include some of these stories in one or other of the collections I've published. Did I keep them out of my books deliberately? I don't think so. I wouldn't have published them if I thought that they were poor work. In each case I can see why I wrote the story, why I did the piece this way instead of that. But I can also perceive in the case of at least two of them that the basic idea of the piece was fundamentally unsuited to my imagination, that maybe I shouldn't have written the story at all. Every artist from time to time realizes, looking back over a long period of work, that certain ideas apparently appropriate to the artistic means available were not in fact suitable to those means. We all lumber ourselves now and then with conceptions that would be better handled by somebody else. Mozart sometimes tries to write like Haydn or Bach, not always with the happiest results. When Beethoven tries to write like Mozart, as in the early quintet for piano and winds, Op. 16, he puts too much strain on the available means and produces an insignificant pastiche. This is a lesson only to be learned by trial and error. In these twelve stories I see myself trying to write like me, but sometimes deviating into trying to write like somebody else, Isak Dinesen or Hemingway, and sometimes trying to do something that you simply can't do in prose fiction.

All these ideas were worth trying. Some of them were very

fruitful for me as I worked through more than seventy stories between 1957 and 1969. I was doing six or seven stories annually besides masses of other work. Leaving *Around the Mountain* (1967) apart, as a special volume for which a dozen stories were specially designed, these pieces from the late fifties and the sixties formed the mass of material from which I was able to assemble *Flying a Red Kite* (1962) and *The Fruit Man, the Meat Man and the Manager* (1971).

Any of the stories included here might have appeared in either of those collections. All of them have found favour in the eyes of editors, sometimes very distinguished connoisseurs of the story like Whit Burnett or Robert Weaver or John Colombo. *The Fruit Man, the Meat Man and the Manager* was dedicated to Robert Weaver 'with admiration and affection' and *Around the Mountain* to John and Ruth Colombo 'with gratitude.' Robert and John were two of the talented group of editors who created *The Tamarack Review,* unquestionably the most important literary magazine in English Canada for the quarter century 1956-1981. I call this collection *The Isolation Booth* because that was the title of my first published story which appeared in *Tamarack* in the Autumn 1958 number.

In one of our family photograph albums there's a picture of me wearing a grey sports jacket that I wish I had now, holding up the cheque from *The Tamarack Review* for 'The Isolation Booth,' the first money I ever earned from my writing, twenty-eight dollars. The magazine paid at the rate of so much per printed page, four dollars if I remember right. I considered this payment very fair and I was glad to get it. In the snapshot I'm grinning like somebody who has just found out where the body is buried. So they give you money for doing this, do they?

Any discussion of Canadian writing between 1956 and 1981 has to confront the phenomenon of *The Tamarack Review.* In the first issue there appeared Timothy Findley's first story 'About Effie,' written at a time when Mr Findley was still preoccupied with his acting career, unaware that he was to develop into the author of *The Wars* and *Not Wanted on the Voyage.* But Weaver and company knew, oh yes! And they knew about Alice Munro and Dave Godfrey. They published work by Robert Kroetsch. They published me. I had fourteen long prose pieces in the magazine from 'The Isolation Booth' in 1958 to the appearance of the Hugh Hood number of the magazine, Summer 1975, which included a long chapter from *The Swing in the Garden* (the first material from *The New Age / Le nouveau siècle* to be published) a month or two before the book appeared.

This body of material included eight short stories, two long excerpts from novels, a semi-fictional memoir, a pair of essays on Expo 67, and an extensive interview with Robert Fulford that appeared in the special issue devoted to my work, altogether about three hundred pages of closely printed text. I had more work in *The Tamarack Review* than anybody else, something I'm very proud of.

John Colombo was the editor at the Ryerson Press responsible for the production of my first book, *Flying a Red Kite*. This publication was suggested to him and supported in many ways by Bob Weaver, who wrote the promotional copy for the dust-jacket. Looking over the table of contents for that collection I find myself wondering why we didn't include 'The Isolation Booth .' I think my instinct was to include it because it had been my earliest publication, and besides it was a 'media folktale,' a kind of story that I've recurred to often.

There were questions of cost, publishing economics, the size of the book, to be considered. At first we thought we only had space for ten stories, and 'The Isolation Booth' didn't quite make it. Then just before going to press the publishers decided that they could squeeze in eleven stories, but John Colombo wanted a *new* story, not one that had been written five years before, so I finished up a brand-new piece, 'The End of It,' and even I could see that it was a more accomplished work than 'The Isolation Booth' so the new story went in and my first offspring had to wait until now to get into a book.

Of course it's a media folktale, a kind of story that I might almost claim to have invented. Back in the mid-1940s Marshall McLuhan planned to publish an early version of his media studies under the title *The Folklore of Industrial Man*. This work never appeared, but when he published *The Mechanical Bride* in 1951 he used the phrase as a subtitle. I used to hear Marshall discussing the notion in any number of undergraduate and graduate courses round about 1947, 1948, 1949. The idea made a great deal of sense to me. A folk isn't necessarily an uncivilized or 'primitive' village people. A folk might be found in Pittsburgh or Toronto, with its own lore and narrative patterns. The industrial world, and especially the post-industrial, high-tech world of the present, might be seen to have many of the qualities of a supposedly primitive village, a perception which would dictate a complete reappraisal of our concepts of the primitive and the folklike or folkish.

The idea of a folk isn't the same as that of a people, clan, family, tribe or nation. Folkishness, the notion of the folk, found considerable acceptance among the Nazis for whom the term *Herrenvolk* denoted a master-race. The distinguishing mark of the folk would be its *pre-rational, instinctual* cohesiveness, guaranteed by some sort of Lawrentian blood-consciousness. The folk recognize one another at some level of understanding and agreement prior to reason and artistic illumination. Why shouldn't there be a media-folk, even a high-tech folk?

Such a group, its self-awareness formed by powerful communications media and advanced information technology, would create its own folklore, concerned among other things with the close relations that exist among multitudes of viewers of the same TV shows, the soaps, Letterman, Arsenio. Ready access to fax communication makes interpersonal relations easy for this folk. The computer hacker knows everybody's business. Mastery of the use of the computer memory would reinforce the group's sense of itself, even though its population could be numbered almost in billions. An enormous viewing, listening, communicating audience could suddenly assume the character of a folk, with systems of belief and superstition that would earlier have been marked down as 'primitive.'

Many of my stories are attempts to annotate the folklore of media and high-tech society. 'The Glass of Fashion,' 'Who's Paying for This Call?' 'Doubles,' 'Crosby,' 'The Woodcutter's Third Son,' 'None Genuine without This Signature,' and others should be noted in this connection. 'The Isolation Booth' is typical media folklore, the tale of a human sacrifice. Willis

Fuller, his showbiz Mom, and the hapless TV announcer who tells the story are examples of folkloric character-drawings: a victim or scapegoat, a dragon lady and a half-smart onlooker. I find it exceedingly interesting that the narrator's name is Marshall, a detail I've never noticed before.

Surely the society that invents a space called 'the isolation booth' isn't far removed from the subliminal motivations of the torturers in prisons and camps of one kind or another. I've always shuddered remembering the phrase, yet it was in common use among millions of weekly viewers of big-money TV quiz programmes like 'The $64,000 Question.' What sort of people invents an isolation booth, then confines children in such a place until they retreat into mental breakdown? The close parallels between media/high-tech culture and pre-rational, instinctual 'blood-consciousness' are obvious. They have continued to increase in significance during the thirty-five years since I wrote 'The Isolation Booth'!

I always try in my stories to maximize the implications of the represented action and the language I happen to be using. All narrators do this, whether Victorian sages, modernists or post-modernists. Speech and action are what you've got going for you. Present-day narrative theories reject what they consider the excessively controlled, tightly planned aesthetic structure of the modernist story, in favour of the open-ended, asymmetrical, unpredictable, sometimes meaningless recounting of incident, often in an invented lexicon something like baby-talk.

Like the modernist however, the post-modernist tries to creep up on extraordinary significance and surprise it into the open. Party membership in an aesthetic movement doesn't confer any right to aesthetic irresponsibility. Narration has its unalterable laws. 'The Perfect Night' is a failure because it violates a fundamental artistic law, one that Henry James, to give only one example, was keenly aware of. Never try to tell somebody else's story! I got the idea from a reading of *Seven Gothic Tales*; in one of these strange pieces a pair of guilty lovers are surprised in each other's arms by terrifying death, the deliberate cruelty of an absolute ruler who buries them alive while they are sleeping, pleased to think that they will awake in the posture of love to discover their fate. What will happen to their sexual attachment as the realization hits them? This narrative suggestion terrified and fascinated me. I tried to do something with it in 'The Perfect Night' but I just wasn't as tough-minded as Baroness Blixen. I copped out, making the lovers' drowning accidental. That spoiled the story.

'The Winner,' written a year later, may be more successful in eluding the requirements of the strictly planned modernist story. It's a series of variations on the religious notion that riches, even accidentally acquired, carry certain ultimate penalties with them. 'How hardly shall a rich man enter the kingdom.' A man, a musician, embeds his life in the values and activities of a religious community, 'a blessed band of saints, the Salvationist Marching Silver Band of the First Company,' and then unthinkingly violates its primordial rules for conduct. He is expelled from the sole institution that gives his life meaning. 'He had never felt so wealthy.' There is a consistent attempt in the writing to imitate the language of the oral fabulist, not a wholly successful undertaking. The story only appeared about twenty years after I wrote it, in a fugitive literary magazine appropriately called *Jubilee*.

A writer in the position I'd been marking out for myself must attempt fable. If 'The Isolation Booth' is media-folk, and 'The Perfect Night' a confused try at the Gothic, fable and the fabulous will come next. All these early pieces are variants, spinoffs as we say today, from the conventional story for the little magazine, ca. 1960. They seem more suitable to today's literary climate than to the age in which I wrote them. They sometimes seem inconsequential or pointless, but at least they don't set up some obvious epiphanic point and crawl slowly towards it through a thicket of literary allusion. It's true that 'The Fable of the Ant and the Grasshopper' refers in multiple ways to James Joyce and Henry James and James Thurber (I seem to have Jacobean reference lodged in my brain) but the action of my fable and its declared moral appealed strongly to a deep strain of anarchism I sense in myself. I approve of the gang of grasshoppers' drinking up Oscar Ant's liquor, and I really dig that moral, 'Never oppress the shiftless and the idle; they may have powerful friends.' This fable was at length published by the distinguished man of letters Mike Gnarowski in his little magazine *Yes* about five years after I wrote it. It seems to have offended many Canadian readers who instinctively felt themselves on the side of the ants. I'm for the grasshoppers myself, and so apparently was Mike Gnarowski.

In those days I'd try any device that seemed likely to deepen out my narrative and give it additional dimension. 'I'm Not Desperate' was written in January 1960, only a day or two after I'd completed the much better-known 'After the Sirens,' which has been anthologized all over the world. 'After the Sirens' was easy to write and became a readers' favourite as soon as it appeared. 'I'm Not Desperate' took a bit longer to find publication, then only in a magazine which ceased publication after three issues, so my story found virtually no audience. It seems to me at least as interesting a narrative as 'After the Sirens.' It's a straight unvarnished piece of serious parody, an attempt to reproduce the musical sound, the sonority, of Hemingway's dialogue from about the period of *The Sun Also Rises*. I found in writing 'I'm Not Desperate' that a writer's deepest inner preoccupations are the sources of his or her style. It is useless, pointless, to impose a superficially realized style on matter alien to it. Any people I can invent will not sound like Hemingway's characters; perhaps it's too bad, but there it is.

> 'I don't know,' he said, 'I'm honourable. I try never to do anything willingly that I think is wrong. I'm virtuous.' He looked embarrassed. 'That sounds crazy, doesn't it?'
>
> 'I don't know,' I said, 'it sounds like a lot of things.'

Hemingway's people might have similar reflections but they wouldn't voice them quite like that, message and medium differently adjusted.

You can't squeeze your own impulses and perceptions into alien language, tone or medium. Sometimes you make wrong decisions about the form the narrative should take. 'Friends and Relations' might be an example of this; the story has had a peculiar history. I tried it on the editors of *Esquire* when I wrote it in the summer of 1960, but they considered it a bit too brief, perfunctory, over-simple, in a word, unacceptable. I put it away for a year or so. Then in 1962, not long after I'd moved to Montréal, I got a letter from the television director and film-maker Paul Almond, saying that he was interested in my work and wondered if I'd like to take some time off from prose to see if I had the makings of a writer for television or the big screen. Had I any script material to show him?

I got 'Friends and Relations' out of the files, half-suspecting that the story might make a TV play. I got hold of a book which showed how to lay out a TV script, audio on one side of the page, video on the other. Without doing much adaptation except to change a place name or two and a couple of characters' names I typed up the story in the form of a one-hour play for television and sent it off to Paul Almond. A little while later the script came back from the director with a very courteous note saying that as it stood this script was completely unproducible for television, but that I wrote good clear dialogue and with much practice might develop into a producible TV writer. I replied that I was probably going to do better at prose fiction than anything else and that I thought I'd better stay with that medium, and that was that. The TV version joined the original story in the files.

Ten years later, around 1973, I got a letter from Fletcher Markle, then head of TV drama at CBC TV, saying that the network was planning a prime-time series called 'The Play's the Thing' to be written by a selection of well-known Canadian fiction writers, Robertson Davies, W.O. Mitchell, Alice Munro, among others. Did I have any TV script material that might be usable in this connection? The network would pay an initial fee of $500 for the chance to examine any such material, and a further, much larger fee for any script actually produced.

Money for jam, I thought. I dug my almost forgotten TV version of 'Friends and Relations' out of a drawer and sent it off to Fletcher Markle. In about ten days I got a cheque for $500 in the mail, with a letter from Markle stating that the network loved the script and would produce it in their series. And so they did. And I didn't have to change as much as a comma of my script! The only thing they asked me to do was to write a very brief (three or four lines) bridging scene – I don't think it involved any dialogue – to link two bits of script material. The 'unproducible' script was produced exactly as written, on the CBC network in an attractive set specially built for the production, starring Maxine Miller and Frank Perry, with a top director, Eric Till, under the ministrations of George Jonas as executive producer. I was very surprised. I had obviously misconceived the narrative material as a piece of prose when it was infinitely more suited to televisic presentation. 'Televisic' is a word I invented, standing in the same relation to TV production as 'cinematic' to film, and 'dramatic' to the stage. 'Televisic' is in fact a word which describes something quite distinct from the essence of either the stage or the cinema.

Anyway, chalk one up for the good guys who knew better than I did what the story should be used for. This TV script found its way into a couple of anthologies intended for educational use. At my suggestion the first of them printed the text of the original story beside that of the TV script. I'm not sure that this excited any special reactions from students but it seemed a sensible thing to do. A more recent anthology, *Front Row: An Anthology of Plays*, Scarborough: Nelson Canada, 1984, reprinted the playscript with four large handsome photographs of the TV show, which enhanced its presentation in the anthology very much. This collection included works both for the stage and for TV, without making any distinction among them. This makes me ponder the possibility of somebody's mounting 'Friends and Relations' on the stage. The critic Pat Morley says that she considers the play an admirable early case of feminist writing, another instance of an observer seeing things in your work that you don't grasp yourself. If anybody out there is looking for a feminist play to produce, I wish she'd (or he'd) give me a call. Perhaps there's something in the script nobody has yet managed to articulate.

This kind of thing happens all the time as narratives are switched from one medium to another. 'Suites and Single Rooms, with Bath' was written in direct response to a request from Bob Weaver for a story specifically for radio broadcast by a single live speaking voice. It's the only story I've ever written for that medium. I've written one or two other stories to be performed by myself at readings, most notably 'God Has

Manifested Himself unto Us as Canadian Tire,' but I'm not a performance artist. Almost all my work is designed to be read silently by very intelligent and attentive readers, a large majority of them women, three or four times. The superb radio actor Budd Knapp read 'Suites and Single Rooms' on air, if my recollection is correct. He brought out all kinds of nuances in the text by pauses, shifts in emphasis, alterations in pitch, that I had not realized were in the story. I wish I had a tape of that reading.

Over a decade later it occurred to me that 'Suites and Single Rooms, with Bath' might also be available to silent reading. I wanted to find out if readers, encountering the piece in print, would suspect that it had been written for solo voice. Would readers miss the effect of the pauses, shifts in emphasis or pitch? If you subtracted the effect of performance would the story be disfigured? I still don't know the answer to any of these interesting questions. The story appeared in *Queen's Quarterly,* Autumn 1972, admittedly a magazine with a limited if select circulation. Not one reader ever recorded any reaction of this kind with me or the editors of the quarterly. Do readers notice points of this kind or do they not? Sometimes the writer labours mightily to bring off some subtle and beautiful formal effect that goes totally unnoticed by the most friendly and enthusiastic readers.

An earlier story for *Queen's Quarterly,* 'A Season of Calm Weather,' tries something I've always wanted to do, that is, to bring to a verbal surface certain mental processes that are in their nature sub-verbal, *below* speech, like musical thought or metaphysical reflection or really intense sexual experience. D.H. Lawrence tries to embody profound sexual feeling in spoken language. I don't think he succeeds in the attempt and I'm not certain that musical or metaphysical or mathematical thought is accessible to narrative. The only true representation of purely musical experience is the music itself. Metaphysical and mystical writing seem to maim the reality there represented. Socrates significantly wrote nothing. Our Lord wrote nothing; five geniuses wrote His life story instead. I've tried now and then to present musical thought in fiction. 'Doubles' is the test case; there's a certain musicality in the story's images and in the sound of some of the wording, but is this the way a great singer / songwriter experiences his music?

Mendelssohn and Mozart could write down a finished piece of music without having made any sketches, that is, in the first draft. They had the music in their heads, as we say. Did they hear it the way we hear it in performance? Was it silently audible, so to speak? How loud was it, how much bass? Did they think musically at some inaudible and even unconscious level, then copy out what some interior impulse dictated? Does anybody know the answer to this? It seems a variation on the psychologists' old inquiry about imageless thought. How do theologians and metaphysicians think? By some process of inner verbalization? Do they talk metaphysics or theology, or mathematics for that matter, to themselves? I don't know, but in 'A Season of Calm Weather' I was trying to get inside the head of a phenomenologist and metaphysician (if there can be such a being) and all I had to do it with were mere visible facts. Maybe it can't be done. Which are the great stories about musicians and metaphysicians and mystics? Are there any?

Other kinds of experience can be equally problematic for writers of fiction; they can turn out to be too factual, too 'given,' for the intensely personal art of fiction. 'The Changeling' is an instance of the struggle between the anecdotal and the literary. I heard something in a casual conversation about a man whom I knew slightly, who had roused an associate from sleep and put him on a plane for Central America without giving him time to wake up fully, finally leaving him stranded in an unknown airport without funds or any knowledge of foreign languages. My God, I thought, that's really, really *picaresque!*

I built 'The Changeling' around that judgement, placing the literary concept of the picaresque in the first paragraph, giving the story a title with a literary allusion, to Middleton's Jacobean play and to fairytale and folklore. My picaro is a man who thinks he's been changed in the cradle by a gypsy band. All this is to fudge the original anecdote with an icing of allusion which obscures the fundamental narrative issues. Postmodernist theorists condemn the allusiveness of the fictions of modernism as *vieux jeu* and insupportable, which they aren't in the hands of a Joyce. Such a theorist would be correct to cite 'The Changeling' as a story based on actuality and obscured by allusion.

Problems of distinguishing anecdote from literary design, at the same time making them reciprocally supportive, perplex the writer of memoirs. Is 'The Ingenue I Should Have Kissed but Didn't' memoir, fiction, reportage, autobiography? The form – if it is a form – is a slippery, uneasy one. Trying to get it adjusted correctly is like trying to nail gelatin to the wall, the matter keeps slithering away from you. Do you use the real names of persons who figure in your story? If not, why not? In 'The Ingenue' I used Bill Hutt's real name, but the real-life Kate Reid comes on as 'Betty Reilly.' If you ask me why, all I can say is that this device seemed appropriate when I wrote the story. Why again? Because the Betty Reilly stuff was very personal? Maybe. The same collection of anecdote dealing with actors and the stage bubbled away in my head for years, finally providing the underpinning for a much more extended treatment of acting, actors, the histrionic and the dramatic, in *The Scenic Art,* which forms Volume Five of *The New Age*.

Writing those early quasi-memoir, autobiographical pieces pushed me in the direction of the kind of meta-fiction attempted in my serial novel where fact, recollection, and the purest imaginative discovery seem to co-exist more comfortably. Bill Hutt is Bill Hutt, Betty Reilly is Kate Reid, and Adam Sinclair is himself and nobody else.

Other, less grave, technical points kept cropping up in those days. 'Educating Mary' proposes the interesting matter of titles and how to choose them, and what to think when virtually the same title used by another writer becomes an international success. Titles are in the public domain; they can't be copyrighted; many of them quote the Bible or Shakespeare anyway. I wrote 'Educating Mary' in July 1964, thinking this title exactly suited to the story of a man, vain, not very brave, who has led a sheltered life and suddenly finds himself face to face with a young and vigorous woman who has intentions which involve him. He isn't educating her; she's educating him. The closing lines state the narrator's alarm at this possibility.

That's an excellent story idea; it's the *point de départ* of the legends about Galatea, to give only one example. I thought my handling of the story was sufficiently original. I liked the story when I wrote it, and I still like it and am pleased to give it an outing in this collection.

But now twenty years go by and 'Educating Rita' becomes a big hit on the London and New York theatrical scene, and then in the funny and touching movie starring Michael Caine and Julie Walters. It's basically the same story as mine. Man thinks he's bringing up young woman who is really opening his eyes to life. And there's my nice title and story idea overlain by another writer's big success so that nobody can read my piece without filtering it through the mesh of the stage and screen success. I have no complaints about this; we all fish in the same pond. I'm just noting my priority with the title for the record. Half a dozen people have written novels called *You Cant Get There from Here,* some with the apostrophe, some without.

So much depends in writing, as in art generally, on *when you're doing it*. In the last twenty years I've evolved to the point where I write stories in clusters of four in the months from September through December; this suits some mysterious inner need which surfaced in the late sixties, probably because I was feeling the strong undertow of *The New Age / Le nouveau siècle*. I had a couple of novel ideas to dispose of, *A Game of Touch, You Cant Get There from Here,* then I could start on the big book. How to keep time free for stories? For a few years I didn't write many of them; then I learned to separate stories from novels, fall and winter / spring.

In the fall of 1966 I was already starting to get a lot of ideas for *The New Age*. I was working on two other novels. I'd try to get four stories written from September to December. I wrote the first one in September all right, 'The Fruit Man, the Meat Man and the Manager,' one of my favourites. Then in the first week of October I got through a first draft of 'The Granite Club,' the closing story in this collection. But while I was in the middle of rethinking the story before a final draft I got the breathtaking news that I'd had two books accepted for publication the following year. Wow! Any writer will tell you what a thrill that gives you, especially at the outset of a writing career.

The books were *Around the Mountain* and *The Camera Always Lies,* a collection of stories and a novel. One book taken by a new young Toronto publisher, the other by a famous, old-established New York house, Harcourt, Brace, publishers among others of T.S. Eliot and the early Sinclair Lewis.

Harcourt, Brace wanted me to recast *The Camera Always Lies* in straight chronological order instead of the rather Conradian circling layout I'd adopted. I agreed to a quick rewrite with an eye to publication in the following fall season. I started a speedy rewrite right after finishing 'The Granite Club' and I think the impending work on the novel made me take my eye off the ball; the finished treatment of 'The Granite Club' lacked clarity of line. I had wanted to tell the story by what the characters didn't say and didn't even think, but the narrative voice is uncertain and hesitant. I put the material aside for another look later on.

And then one evening in Fredericton NB about five years later, I met John Moss, Dave Arnason, Mel Dagg, and some other graduate students who were starting *The Journal of Canadian Fiction.* I liked their idea for a new literary quarterly, which eventually began publication and became one of the influential voices of the 1970s and early 1980s. The editors asked if I'd care to submit a story for the first number. Anybody who is interested will find 'The Granite Club' in JCF 1, No. 1 (Winter 1972) next to a fine piece by Gail Fox, 'The Cause for War.' I was pleased to be represented there and I don't think 'The Granite Club' looks out of place in that context. In the end the reader must always be the one who decides, so why not let me know what you think sometime? Do you understand what's happening in 'The Granite Club'?

Be warned! Even if you don't let me hear from you I have my spies everywhere. I have ways of knowing what you decide, and believe me, I'm listening.

The Isolation Booth

The Isolation Booth

THIS WAS A NICE little guy – no, I'm not being funny – he was a sweet kid when he first made the programme. He played the banjo and sang all those songs from the twenties and thirties. He could do a lot of cute tricks and looked very engaging so we decided to use him. You can see that we had to be careful.

Our ratings had been skidding. We subscribed to Neilsen and Trendex. Neilsen had us slumping and we were barely holding our own with Trendex. The thing was, we had too many imitators. We were first with the idea, but the other shows were cutting into us badly. So we'd been using a lot of gimmicks, grannies who bet two bucks daily at Jamaica, cops who read Schopenhauer – we couldn't use authentic experts because there was no switch value. An expert ought to be able to handle his own specialty, after all. We tried to find entertaining personalities who just happened to know funny things. The audience could feel that they were real folks except for the special hobby. I was up to my derrière in just plain folks.

We hadn't been sold on using a child – or at least we'd have used one any time we could get hold of a good one. There were vast hordes of teeny moppets trying to crash the programme, or their mothers were trying, or somebody was – the Big Guy in the Sky, I don't know. But the first prodigies who were interviewed were little pricks – one and all – snotnoses, and their mothers were worse. They were all being driven and driven – the kids, I mean – which meant that the first upset would crucify them. On a show like ours, with thirty million eyeballs fixed on you, you don't do the Como bit unless you happen to be Perry. I don't come out and rub my cheek and I've had thirty years in the business. Sometimes when a contestant is fishing around for a money answer you can sense what's shrivelling his gut. It isn't the most comfortable sensation.

They're bumpkins, mind you. They're clods trying to grab an easy buck, and when they find out how tough that easy buck is, just for getting up there on TV, they start to bleed. On the whole I don't much like our contestants. One or two, yes. They acted like professionals and they knew we had a show to do. But mainly they're a bunch of grasping suckers. They're sweet; they're real folks.

I was telling you about Willis. Willis Weston Fuller and his banjo. Henry came over to me one afternoon during rehearsal with a huge grin pasted on his face.

'Looks pretty tight, Mr Leland,' he said, using the Percy Kilbride voice; he does it at parties.

'It's tight enough,' I told him, 'as long as Granny Gates doesn't wet her pants when she announces her decision.'

'You don't think she will?'

'Relax, Henry,' I said. 'I'll keep her calm.'

'Marshall,' he said, 'you're the best MC in the trade.'

'I know it.'

'And I've got a present for you just to show how much I like your work.'

'Henry,' I said, 'if you don't mind, I better finish the rehearsal.'

'You can take a few minutes; you're a big star. Let them set the lights. Listen, I've found a kid we can use. You'll love him.'

'I love all our guests. You know that.'

'Absolutely. But you'll *really* love him.'

'How old is he?' I'd told Henry definitely I wouldn't even look at anybody under the age of puberty. Adolescents I can just swallow, but I call a halt at full-fledged moppets.

'Fourteen, I believe.'

'What's his line?'

'Popular songs of the twenties and thirties.'

'What does a kid that age know about the twenties and thirties?'

'This one knows everything. You'd be surprised.'

'You figure he'll go for dough?'

'I honestly do.'

'I'll see him at the office in the morning.'

'You're a good boy, Marshall.' He got out of the way and the rehearsal went on. You know Henry – a good idea man, not too practical, they never are. Still, he seemed to be right about Willis. I talked to the boy and his mother the next day, and while she was the usual Medusa, he was a damned good-looking youngster. Nice speaking voice. Spoke up clearly to everything I asked him. He didn't seem to be afraid of me, which is a bit unusual. After all, I was getting to be quite the little celebrity. I took the office's word that he knew his subject. He played his banjo and sang for me and frankly wasn't bad at all. A small voice, mind you, but enough to pick up. He looked so good and we'd wanted a kid with appeal for so long that we jumped him right onto the big show. His first time out we were running pretty late but we squeezed in ninety seconds to fool around and show him off.

'Willis,' I said laughingly, 'your category is tunes of the twenties and thirties. How did you pick them up? You weren't around then, were you?' Small chuckle from audience.

'That's where the good banjo tunes come from, Mr Leland. I picked them up learning the banjo.'

'Could you give us a quick chorus before we get on to your question? I know everyone would like to hear you.' And you know what? He did it. We hadn't rehearsed it because we were tight, but he took off on his banjo like he'd been on TV all his life. He did a chorus of 'I'm Just Wild About Harry' and the audience loved it. Then we did the easy questions and he went through them like a house afire, right up to the first plateau without taking a breath. Eleanor interrupted us then, but it didn't matter because he couldn't have gone any further that week anyway.

'All right, Willis,' I told him. 'You go home and think about it and next week come back and tell us what you want to do. Your category will be limited to Broadway hits by Cole Porter.' Then I had to segue fast into the close commercial. It was a good entertaining half-hour and we got very good Trendex on it. We'd needed a rating, let me tell you. We began to get mail encouraging him and telling us not to make the questions too hard.

It was nearly the same on his next appearance. Besides Willis we had two other people coming along who had big appeal and we looked set for good ratings well into the next month. We moved Willis into the lead-off slot. We always put the big jackpot in the second fifteen minutes so that the show had a story-line. Somebody coming fast to open. Then your big money-man. Then a new face to close. So we had him leading off and we began to rehearse him in the booth, which is where I always keep my eyes peeled. You could see he didn't like it inside. It made him very nervous and I'll swear he hadn't been nervous at all originally. I remember something he asked me.

'Can't I take the banjo in with me?'

'No,' I said. 'There's no room and you won't need it.'

'It's lonely,' he said.

Well, you know how it is; they all feel that way at first, but it usually wears off. I told him so, but he didn't seem very reassured. However, in he went.

He didn't quite click the second time out. I don't think the audience felt it, but he didn't have the spontaneity. His answers to my friendly questions weren't coming back with any snap, the way they had in rehearsal. We tried to work the intimate friendly bit, but he was too stiff to establish it. He was letting his eyes wander all around the theatre, which is bad. I'd warned him about that. Once or twice I had to drive my line at him to get him to answer and this made me a little uncomfortable. Still and all I got him into the booth. He could work the control buttons and knew where to direct his voice, but he had a bad case of the fidgets. The whole situation seemed a bit out of line; and then of course his question was a whole lot tougher.

He answered it okay – six obscure ballads from primeval Porter shows, not the kind of thing you'd be likely to do on the banjo. I got him out of there quick and we did the song. The whole sequence had gone too fast. We might have wasted a minute, but could he stand an ad-lib? Who knows? And naturally he flubbed the second chorus. I nodded towards the Teleprompter and he just stood there.

I carried it off – old Marshall, veteran of stage and screen. 'Lose a line somewhere, Willis?'

'Gosh, Mr Leland,' he stuttered, 'I just can't recall –'

'Never mind,' I told him. 'That isn't part of your question.' I got him off pretty well. All the same, we weren't relaxing together, which made me wish he'd take his winnings and quit. No such luck though. Next day he and his mother came down to the office and insisted on sitting in on the production meeting, which of course nobody had ever done before, although I guess they had a right to be there. While Mrs Fuller was making a host of valuable suggestions, the boy sat there watching her and looking more and more uncomfortable. I noticed that he was carrying a book called *Principles of Television Production* which she'd given him as a prop. He didn't make any special use of it.

It was clear that he was staying with us and though we never, but never, interfered with the contestants, I felt disturbed about the decision. We never even talked to them outside rehearsals, you know. Somebody might claim the whole deal was faked. I was surprised when Willis began to get very chummy with me during the last rehearsal before that week's show. After we'd done our lines together he grabbed my arm.

'Marshall,' he said, very self-assured, 'you're a great help to me.' I had to stop and look at him.

'What did you say?'

'I said you're a great help.'

'No, no. Before that.'

He looked puzzled. 'Do you mean "Marshall"?'

'That's what I mean,' I said. 'Now, listen, Willis, I'm thirty years older than you. I'm not one of your buddy-boys at school. And while we're working together we'll just keep things on a 'Mister Leland' basis, eh?'

'I was just trying to be friendly.'

'There's a difference between being friendly and being too big for your pants. I mean that.' At that he wilted and didn't say anything more. Afterwards I felt lousy I'd taken him up so short, but it had been a lousy week and you have to draw the line somewhere.

On the show we did the usual dialogue which he went through pretty well until I asked him if he was going for the next money. Then there was this horrible minute of dead air; he didn't say a word and an odd expression came over his face. I glanced at the monitor and caught sight of Mrs Fuller on the screen. She was sitting in the audience hunched way forward in her seat with the same strange look on her face. She gave me a queer sensation like she was looking over my shoulder. I pulled myself together and put the question to him again, louder. All at once he came out of it and said that yes, he was going ahead.

We got him into the booth and you could see that he was shaking like a leaf; you could even see perspiration. The camera crew, the dopes, pulled in close at exactly the wrong time. They timed it so that everybody in the country saw how he was reacting. As soon as the director got a peek at the monitor he cut to me and didn't shoot Willis again until he absolutely had to. By this time the harm had been done.

Oh sure! Sure he answered the question, but not until I repeated parts of it several times; it almost looked like he was stalling for a hint. I don't know how much the office tells them, but I was damned careful ever since I gave a contestant an answer without thinking. I nearly lost my job right there, so I took plenty of care not to give Willis or anybody else any free tip-off. No hints from me.

Actually he knew the answer. I never had any complaint about his knowing the answers; as far as that goes he was a very good contestant. He finally came through on this one and eased out of the booth in pretty rocky shape. A stage-hand came over, nearly on camera, to hand him his banjo and he just stared at the guy stupidly. Then he looked at the banjo as if he didn't know what it was for. He'd been pencilled in tentatively to sing, but it was no time for merry song. I improvised some small talk.

'You're getting close, Willis. Nearly over now. One more week. I'll bet that makes you feel good.' I had to speak sharply to wake him up.

'Oh,' he mumbled, 'oh, I don't know.'

'Willis,' I said. 'Could you speak a bit louder? We're not picking you up.'

He was in shock. He looked at me vaguely and said: 'Huh?'

'Could you speak a bit louder? The audience can't hear.'

'The audience,' he muttered. 'They don't know what it's like.' Luckily nobody could hear this last gem; he swallowed it. I grabbed his arm then and steered him up the runway good and fast. I had to walk off camera leaving us with an empty set, and of course Henry had plenty to say about that. We finished that little outing with a new face who looked like he could handle himself, a fortyish professor of economics whose subject was 'All the Fish in the Sea'. A very hard customer, frankly trying to make money out of us. You could see that he wasn't going to lose control of himself at the sight of the big bundle. He made me feel at ease and that's a real switch. I was glad when things were over.

That last week we got tons of mail from viewers all over the country telling us we were making a nervous wreck out of a little child for sordid commercial purposes. We were inhuman monsters. The Society for Prevention of Cruelty to Kiddies ought to be urged to fight the case, and so on. Henry complained about this bitterly.

'I can't understand it,' he kept saying. 'We give the kid more money than he'll earn in the next fifty years and the public hates us.' He was very disturbed, shocked, and disappointed.

'They're just working off repressions,' I reassured him. 'They can't hurt us. We've got a signed release from his mother, haven't we?'

'Yes, but would it hold up in court?'

'Cut it out, Henry. Nothing's coming into court. We haven't done anything to him.'

'I hope you're right,' he said. 'I can't understand the little jerk at all. He looked so good at his interviews.' He wandered off somewhere to worry.

We kept soft-pedalling it with Willis even when he tried to tell the director how he wanted the cameras handled, this close-up here, that medium shot there. It began to get pretty nauseating, but there was only one more week and he was a hundred and fifteen pounds of Trendex; he was our rating. So we got down to showtime without actual violence. I opened with our economics professor, all about cephalopods; it was rich, human and warm. I calmed down a bit and we went into the centre commercial dead on time. Then we got to Willis and you know what happened.

On he came, looking just as appealing as he had in the beginning. We chatted, quite friendly, and then I asked him if he was going to go for it. All I could do was wait; I had detailed instructions.

'I guess so,' he said, very low.

I had to get him to repeat it: 'Are you going to continue?'

'I better ...' As the stagehands pushed the booth into position he caught sight of it. Eleanor came over to put him in and he jerked his arm away from her. She's a nice girl.

'No,' he said. 'No. I'm not going in there. No.' His voice began to rise.

'Willis!' I said, trying to get a word in, but it was useless.

'I won't go in. I've changed my mind. I won't do it. Nothing can make me do it.' He had started to shout and all of a sudden he was crying. I signalled the director to cut away fast, so they shot the studio audience on Three which was no better because they were all on their feet ready to storm the Bastille. They cut back to Willis for a horrible second and he was screaming and completely gone. Then they decided on a shot – a long long close-up – of me. Standing there with nothing to say for almost a minute. I found out next day when the agency men made me sit through a kine. You can imagine the good *that* did me.

The stagehands helped the kid off and he was screaming all the way. He still hadn't come out of it. Something, I don't know what, woke me up and I did an ad-lib speech about how surprised and upset we all were. I told them how much we liked young Willis and how he could keep the money he'd won already and how we knew he'd be okay after a night's sleep. Then we were running late and I had to come off. God!

It ruined us. The sponsors, the agency men, and the network fought over the thing for a week and then gave us the axe. Henry's all right, the bastard; he has two other shows. But that was my only network affiliation. Now all I'm doing is this lousy daytime seg locally and nobody sees me. I've been needing extra money so I got Chuck to fix me up with a couple of courses in the Department of Speech and Drama at Columbia. And who do you think was the first person I saw when I walked into the classroom? Yeah! Mrs Fuller. God damn it, she's my best student – she's got million angles. And she wants me to help her get started in TV when she's finished her courses. I suppose I could, but honest to God, I'm afraid to.

The Perfect Night

IT WAS, beyond a doubt, a perfect night, the sky overhead and all the warm blanket of air a velvety black. There was no cloud cover and the moon shone on the water with a steady brilliant light, streaking the almost imperceptible rise and fall of the sheltered basin with alternate yellow and black. In the basin, the six-ton cruising yawl *Debutante* pulled steadily and easily at her mooring as the flood began to rise and stream past her up-channel.

Debutante was a sound, comfortable sea-boat, aging now and a trifle under-canvassed but extremely handy in all weathers. Her rigging was simple – classical – and very manageable so that a crew of three might handle her easily at all times. In ordinary circumstances, two could manage and even if one of them should find it necessary to go below to prepare a meal a single man could carry on by himself for a considerable time. Just now the yawl carried an amateur crew of three, her owner, his wife, and their friend, the scholar Arthur Brome, on a holiday coasting cruise.

It was long past midnight. Keeping the harbour watch, midnight to eight, which the three amateurs took in turn when they were in port, was *Debutante's* wealthy owner, Henry Harley. He lolled comfortably at his ease in the roomy cockpit, loving the quiet of the night; he had slept earlier and had come on deck just before midnight, sending the others below for a good night's sleep – they hoped to do another hundred miles or so tomorrow, the last day of their holiday. Harley had checked the mooring lines an hour ago, before slackening them slightly to allow for the flood, and now he was enjoying his first pipe of the watch. Apart from the yawl's lights, the glow of his pipe's coal was all that might be seen of life, aboard the yawl, from even a very short distance away.

Harley wore a pair of old duck trousers, much patched and mended, a sweater rolled at the neck, and a dirty cap. He had grown to know these clothes by years of use. Now they fitted him like a second skin – he scarcely realized that he had them on. At his office in town he wore expensive neckties and shirts whose collars made the pulse in his throat flutter annoyingly.

From time to time he stared at his pipe's coal, or at the yacht's tiny lights, with a peculiar intensity, as though he meant to extract some obscure information from their discreet glow. But most of the time he let his eyes roam in the darkness without making any effort to pierce the velvet night. He had the moonlight above him, after all, and no harm could come to his craft on a beautiful night like this.

He let his eyes and his mind wander together in the darkness, deliberately refusing to permit either apparatus to focus for very long. Now and then he stared around the cockpit, at the open forward hatch where a darker patch of black led to the owner's cabin in which his wife lay perfectly still, quite nude because of the air's warmth, sound asleep, and sometimes at the rear hatch below in which his friend Brome lay, neither still nor sound asleep.

Brome tossed and turned and occasionally emitted a troubled snore. But from the forward cabin no such sound emerged. Miranda never snored; no faintly ridiculous infirmities marred the perfect surface of her life. Harley moved quietly forward to adjust the sliding hatch above his sleeping wife's head, fixing it wider open. He was careful not to disturb her and he hoped that neither cabin was too stuffy; there was very little breeze.

He considered going below to be certain that his crew could sleep comfortably but decided against it; he did not particularly care to examine Miranda's flawless naked untroubled form, asleep as she was. Much better to stay on deck and draw quietly on his pipe. He was alone and quiet and preferred to stay that way, for he had been made too much to feel the inconvenience of his presence during this short cruise. If there was no one awake on the yawl whom his presence would – not 'offend,' that was too strong – but rather 'deter,' yes, that was it, deter, let him enjoy the unfamiliar luxury of deterring no one. It is not pleasurable to be a husband too frequently in the way. And a six-ton yawl provides very little space to move about in.

Henry Harley knew very well that if he had passed the night

ashore the harbour watch would have been kept only by the gulls and the riding-lights. And the after-cabin would have been left untenanted.

Though he was a rich and powerful man, and, he supposed, a fool, he could not find in his heart any storm of recrimination or any feeling of betrayal. For he had long understood their situation, the three of them and all the others, when they had undertaken the holiday cruise.

'Arthur's so inconvenient, darling. Shouldn't we ask someone else?'

'Arthur will do, Miranda. He knows how to read a chart.'

It was a small accomplishment that none of the others possessed.

He sighed and stretched and went on listening to the occasional snore and the 'slap-slap' of the water against the hull and as he did so he became aware, almost imperceptibly at first, and then more and more insistently, of the sound of a gasoline engine somewhere nearby. It seemed quite close at times, and at times farther off, but sound is notoriously deceptive over bodies of water and he couldn't at first locate the source accurately. He wondered who it might be, for he and his yawl were relative strangers to this part of the coast and he was uncertain of the customs of the natives. He gazed about him as the drumming of the motor grew somewhat louder and nearer, as it seemed, trying to guess whose boat this might be; it sounded like an inboard launch. At length he made out a more solid small patch of black, moving slowly nearer to him. As it approached he concluded that it was the boat of some local official; he was perfectly right.

'On board the yawl ...' said a pleasant, cheerful voice, interrogatively and surprisingly quietly. Harley wondered what was wrong.

'Can you ease closer?' he asked, speaking in his normal level tone. 'Everyone's asleep.'

His invisible interlocutor laughed quietly at this. 'We won't disturb your crew,' he said. The launch moved slowly closer, out of the darkness which concealed it. Harley saw a man with a boathook in the stern keeping the launch from colliding with his own craft and then he made out the other person in the launch, the fellow who had spoken to him, who wore a cap with some kind of official badge.

'You had better not stay here,' said this man. By way of explanation he added, politely and almost deferentially, 'I'm the harbourmaster.'

'I moored here with no difficulty,' answered Harley, 'and I don't want to shift my mooring now. What's the trouble?'

'You must have made port after dark.'

'Yes.'

'Did you consult the tide-tables?'

'As a matter of fact, I didn't. There's plenty of water under us.'

'You don't know the harbour then?'

'I haven't been here since before the war.'

'I'm really sorry to bother you,' said the young harbourmaster courteously, 'you'd be all right at almost any other time of the month.'

'Go on.'

'Look at the current, how swift it is. Yesterday, today, and tomorrow are the peak days this month.'

'The moon's to blame,' said Harley wryly, guessing what was coming.

'That's right,' said the harbourmaster, laughing again with a curious carefree note. 'If you stay here there'll be no water under you in the morning. You'll be heeled over at forty-five degree angle on a stinking mud flat. You won't be able to get ashore and it's going to be very warm. And there might be trouble at the next flood. You might not float off too easily.' He was clearly trying to be fair and helpful and Harley appreciated it.

'I see,' he said slowly, 'thank you very much. Should I moor up-channel?'

'Right in the channel a couple of miles up. Nothing heavy comes up that far and you'd be safe there if you drew eighteen feet.' He chuckled. 'I don't expect you do.'

'No.'

'Just work a couple of miles up-channel, out of the traffic. Do you have power?'

'Of course.'

'Then there you are. Good night, sir, and I'm sorry to disturb you.'

'Not at all,' said Harley, 'good night and thank you.'

The launch's engine went into reverse and she slid away into the darkness. He watched her disappear and then gave his attention to his own auxiliary engine. He propped up the engine-housing on its metal arms and was about to turn the engine over when a thought struck him. No need to wake the others with the noise of the auxiliary. He rose and made his way to the forward hatch which he slid quietly closed. He looked at it for moment and then secured it tightly. He did the same with the after hatch, making certain that it was shut tight and concluding that neither Miranda nor Arthur could possibly be disturbed by the sound of the engine. Then he started it up, listening until its initial coughing rough beat smoothed out as it began to warm up. When he was satisfied that power was available, he left the engine on idle and went forward.

The mooring line had grown taut in the last hour. Puffing slightly he tugged at it until he could reach the wet and intractable knot. He recognized one of Miranda's highly idiosyncratic knots, to which only she had the key. After wrestling with it for a few moments he almost concluded that he would have to wake her but suddenly the line twisted like a snake in his hands and the knot disappeared magically; the line came inboard and the current carried *Debutante's* head around.

He felt the hull rise and move forward beneath his feet and, coiling the mooring line and putting it out of the way, he came aft, gave the engine a little gas, and took the wheel.

The current of the flood was still strong and he only needed steerage-way, so he kept the auxiliary cut back as far as he could, and as quiet as possible. The yawl began to move, quickly enough nonetheless, up-channel.

He thought that the moonlight had begun to wane somewhat although there was plenty to steer by. He seemed to be moving between alternate yellow and black stripes, as the water moved under the keel, stripes of moonlight on patches of black water, a curious effect, the narcotic recurrence of light and dark. It was past two o'clock.

Harley was unfamiliar with the harbour and the channel but

he found no difficulty in making his way into very deep water indeed. The slapping sound stopped and a rhythmic gurgle took its place as the yawl slid swiftly through the current. Half a mile off on each side the blacker masses of the hills above the shoreline could dimly be seen. Ahead, only variations in the deepening shadows indicated the bends of the channel as it narrowed and penetrated deeply into the land away from the coast and the outer harbour. He picked his way from stripe of yellow to stripe of yellow, languidly estimating his rate of progress, paying little heed to possible dangers. He didn't even consult the chart, which was lying in a roll on the floor of Arthur Brome's cabin. He had left the business of charts to Arthur. He let the moonlight lead him on.

THEY MUST HAVE been doing at least ten knots over the ground when the shock came. He had been making for what looked like another patch of black between the yellow stripes, completely unaware that this wasn't only water but a jagged shelf of rock, bare even at high tide, carefully indicated on the charts and by a series of buoys which he hadn't bothered to pick up.

With a horrifying rending splintering smash *Debutante* ran on the rock. Her keel broke to one side immediately and she canted sharply over. Harley, who was totally unprepared, was flung over the side. His pipe flew out of his hand, hissing as it extinguished itself in the water. He fell on his side against the flint-like rock, gashing himself dangerously below the ribs. From there he rolled off into deep water.

In an instant he cried out loudly and incoherently, paddled feebly a few yards out into the channel, and tried to make out the figure of his craft. The noise of her destruction continued, and as he realized that she was going to break up in the next minute, he fought back to the shelf, dragged himself onto it slipping in the shallow current that washed over it, and tried to clamber back into the cockpit. He saw with sudden horror that he was too late. Poised on the jagged edge of the shelf *Debutante* was breaking her back. As he struggled to climb up into the cockpit he saw in front of his very eyes an enormous tear appear in the planking. He loosed his hold and tumbled back off the ledge into the channel.

With a terrible sound the yawl split in half across the point of stress below the cockpit and with a noise like an express train the broken halves of the hull slid off on either side of the ledge of rock and sank like stones. He had no idea if there had even been cries.

Above him the gulls cried out, circling invisibly over the twin swirling circles that still moved lazily above the disaster. Helpless in the water, poor Harley sobbed indistinguishably to himself, incapable for the moment of assessing his situation.

He became slowly aware that he was very weak, that if he was to save himself he must move quickly before he lost the last elements of his strength. The water seemed quite warm; it had washed out the tear in his side and almost seemed to have stanched the flow of blood. His sandals had washed away and the trousers were only a slight encumbrance. Much depended on whether or not he could free himself from his sweater, which was clotting and dragging around him as its thick wool became sodden. The sleeves were loose so that he could free his sound arm without too much pain and difficulty but pulling it over his head while he supported himself was terribly dangerous.

He lay quietly on his back gazing at the sky while he measured the risk. It had to be attempted; he would never make it to shore with his shoulders entangled like this. It did not occur to him to pass the remainder of the night on the rock; he felt that however hopeless the situation he should try to get assistance as soon as he could.

He paddled slowly, maintaining his balance with his good arm while with infinite care and great pain he slowly worked the other arm out of its sleeve. Then with the sleeves floating free he worked the heavy sodden choking sweater to his shoulders, praying that he wouldn't become entangled.

Then he suddenly ducked his head backwards, pulling the mass of wool back over his head. It worked. He shook his head free, and rolling on his wounded side, he began a laborious sidestroke toward the shore, a half-mile away. Often he had to lie on his back to struggle against shock and fight for breath and a brief rest. Dawn was beginning to appear eastward in the sky when he made the beach to lie exhausted and terrified on the sand.

After a long time he dragged himself to his feet to gaze at the light in the east. He thought suddenly of Arthur and Miranda with the water squeezing the life out of them, each one alone. He wondered if either one had gained the hatchway to find it tightly closed.

'They'll think I did it! They'll think I meant it!' he cried, bursting into tears. Realizing that he was wet, naked, and badly hurt, he turned, and stumbling, began to run along the beach toward a coast-guard station nearby.

The Winner

BROWN LEAVES FLUTTERED down a dull sky. Surveyed from atop the deserted Ferris wheel, gaunt and still against the dullness, the fairgrounds seemed lifeless, empty exhibition buildings scattered here and there below, narrow vistas proffering prospects of dry fountains, papier-mâché statues lying naked to the gazer – the summer's party over and the excursionists departed.

Once a solitary workman climbed unwillingly, ordered to, bullied into the climb by his foreman, to the top of the Ferris wheel, angling back and forth across its gaunt members, shivering in the October air. Close to the top he halted for a hastily-drawn breath, a hastily-drawn glance at the flat fairgrounds, a feeling in his pockets for nuts and bolts needful for the purposes of this dizzying ascent. Gathering himself, the resentful workman turned again to the climb and at length perched himself legs astraddle in the highest car from whence the broad world curved out falling away on either side to his unconcerned glance.

He fell to his task swinging in the highest car and attempting to arrest its swing through an arc of a hundred degrees in the brisk air. He inserted bolts humming to himself; he flicked his coat collar higher, stretched his legs in the car which was commodious enough for four – it was *such* a Ferris wheel – and now and then he gave his amazed gaze to the huge mushroom at the extremest northernmost reach of the fairgrounds. The tent.

Well might he gaze astonished at this bulging mushroom perched as he was at so propitious an angle of observation. In all the flat dead three hundred and fifty acres, now that the trippers were gone to Buffalo, to Oshawa, to Rome, N.Y., now that the last candy-floss was eaten, all of it, and the last child had vomited, the sucker been gloriously fleeced of his wad, only the tent flourished, no, rather bulged with life on the banks of the grey lake by the fairgrounds.

The workman dropped his monkey wrench, hoping the

foreman stood below it. It'll split his derby, he thought hopefully, it'll crown his fat head. But he only heard the clunk of his wrench splitting itself into parts on the cement parkette below. Then, at a later time, after his many numbed bummed cigarettes, after what the labourer calls a railroad piss – walk a mile and piss an hour – he climbed reluctantly down the girders, watching his footing, and staring as he drew closer to the ground at the bulging ominous mushroom of a tent which so dominated the landscape as one drew down towards it.

From the Ferris wheel the tent seemed just another squashable mushroom though overflowing with juicy life; on the flat ground with empty autumnal vistas and dry fountains all about, it seemed the apotheosis of warm life. From its warm enclave there came shouted song. The Tenth International Congress of Championship Evangelical Silver Bands was meeting there in its pomp.

Consciously, like a sinner before the spying Lord, I say consciously evading the eye, that steely orb, of his inquisitive derbied foreman, that bastard, send a man up that thing in the middle of winter, the workman lingered close by the tent half fearful of the shouted oath drawing him back to the late afternoon's maintenance. It bulged; it burst with full life; many thousands crouched on splintery plank row on row from the ring's circumference, higher and higher to the extreme outer edge under the roof where sat the guilty and the unregenerate sneaking a smoke in direct contravention of the regulations and the Lord on their tough bleacher seats, their backsides shoved tight against the canvas at the high edge of the great mushroom of a tent.

Now at last the *hors-d'oeuvres* were complete; they had chanted the old hymns. Not the spurious rock and roll of a compromising juke-box evangelicalism or the simple jungle Holy Roller fervour but the older finer literate hymns, those of Isaac Watts and the ineffable Baxter, the deist Blackmore, and those of many more writers of the Aufklärung.

They knew not themselves, these bawling hymnsters in their piety, the goodly heritage of their great-grandfathers' grandfathers' rationalism; they only knew a good silver band when they heard one and here assembled were their army's flower, championship silver bands from Great Britain – the Battersea General Booth Regimental – fine bands, good bands from Sydney, Australia. But these were mere aperitif; for the championship band, their own band, a blessed band of saints, a goodly band, the Salvationist Marching Silver Band of the First Company of Chippewa, Ontario, has carried off the prize a third year running and is now to cap the three-day Congress with its most celebrated rendering.

The tender tenor aria from Handel's *Jephtha* transcribed in its majesty for cornet solo and band accompaniment.

A hush. Eight measures of introduction. Then clear and full-toned, nay, brilliant even, comes the sounding cornet, Boosey and Hawkes Ecclesiastical Special, Number 24, to be had, friends, at all music shops where lovers of the horns foregather. A famous cornet, a presentation piece, clear here in the intricate involute vocalizations of the Handel. Oh, he knew how, did old impresario opportunist Handel, how to write for the soloist, how to show off his graces.

What then of our soloist, our kingly cornetist jigging on his bunioned feet in the ring's centre, focal point of full six thousand eyeballs, as he plays mightily for dear life, too much aware, not of the six thousand eyeballs, no, but of those of his leader the Cyclopean bandmaster eyeing him fixedly swinging his swagger stick alert in blue full dress with scarlet facings? 'Tis only under some such authority we come to the centre of the ring at last.

He dances crabwise in the limelight tootling for dear life does our hero, Bandsman Harris Fudger, storied cornetist, a stubby man afraid lest he miss a note of the intricate evolution of the tenor's argument; he teeters on the brink of a run, slides triple-tonguing down while the crowd sits entranced gazing at his stubby limelit figure as the notes spray silverly out to the highest hindermost row where sit the smoking unregenerate, admiring in spite of themselves the most famous band, the most expert cornetist, in the Dominion.

It is a very long exercise with a da capo and a formal tutti for coda, not one clear pause to steal breath, such a designer was old George Frederick writing for tenor and not, as Harris Fudger would gladly tell you one and all, not for cornet.

Anyway he makes his run and jigs more gleefully watching the swagger stick, trying to avoid the thousand eyes of the bandmaster, thinking, ah! dear hearts, of the blue paper in his tunic pocket, waiting for the end of the run, of the solo, of the evening's sawdust affairs, the removing from his swollen lips of the harsh mouthpiece. So his sweet sound comes to an end while the crowd relaxes after counting carefully every note, searching for a sloppy one so as, afterwards over their beer, to condemn the *embouchure* of the storied cornetist. He makes it missing never a note and the crowd sits disappointedly back on its spine, hypercritical, to listen to the tutti.

Now the bandmaster parades his ascendancy and Harris Fudger is forgotten with but sixty-four measures remaining. He jigs uncertainly back and forth in the very last row of the band's array and at length only a poor cold labourer, weak from climbing frozen Ferris wheels in the dead October, sees Harris Fudger turn and scuttle anxiously out of the ranks and away from the massed bands in the arena, and down a row, and out of the ring, palpably looking for a bathroom.

He plans to make this excuse to the bandmaster who, years earlier it seems, has told the musicians that they must not faint, waver on their feet, fall out of line, until, he says with swagger, until your back teeth are afloat. When you gotta go, Harris thinks, it's an excuse after all, you gotta; and I will see you all at band practice next week or at prayer meeting on Sunday or on a street-corner at Christmas; but I am finished here today. I'll tell them all I had to go. And he thinks again and again, as he runs off, of the blue paper in his pocket which impels his flight. He pauses, it is true, in an ammoniac men's room to lend colour to his tale and to satisfy, as the psychologists say, bless them, a felt need.

He pauses not long and looks nor to left nor to right leaving the fairgrounds, but hastens like an arrow from the bow of the god of love north along pedestrian Dufferin Street (how arbitrary is the narrative, bound to the commonplace) to where the crowd awaits him, Jakie Forbes, Alf Pullan and the rest, in the men's beverage room of the Gladstone Hotel.

Oh ye heavenly fair, ye gods, we thank thee in thy wisdom for having first made known to men that chief fruit of the malt and hops. I mean beer, blessed cordial. Thus muses cornetist Fudger, or perhaps not quite thus but near enough, as he scuttles along. And now the cheery electric sign approacheth through the gloom, the foul October vapours and the dank autumnal mists. He draws near. He enters and the warm beeriness laps him round. There are many shouted greetings and he thinks of the blue paper but he realizes his habits are known; there may be a pursuit. So he surrounds himself with a goodly crew, Alf, Jackie, Nolan Alexander, and the waiter.

'What news?' they chorus. 'What news from abroad?'

Cheerily smiles the cornetist, facing them out, good hearts, good fellows all, over the question direct. He knows, does Harris Fudger, of the electrifying potencies of his blue paper, crackling in his tunic pocket. He sounds the waiter who, smiling at his regulars thinking of his interminable series of ten-cent tips, hovers paternally above them, tray at the ready laden with foaming drafts.

Oh, the ten-cent draft beer, the eight-ounce glass, solace of poverty, hope of the inexpensively inebriate, where are you now? How long it seems, the years between, since first we tasted of that ten-cent draft, when a man with two dollars, or perhaps even a dollar and a half, might comfortably cheerily stretch his skin tight and tip the waiter decently, abusing not home and children so inexpensive was his good cheer. Where are you now, old ten-cent glass of beer? We see you not but Harris Fudger sees you, calling for glasses all round, clack clack on the table top they go.

Nolan Alexander, Alf Pullan, Jackie Forbes, Harris Fudger and the others, they lift their glasses and empty them at a swallow. Harris pays.

Clack clack clack again go tumbler bottoms on the table. Casting an eye around him for the supervisor the noble waiter slinks into the men's lavatory where he clack clacks a few for himself, jingling his tips cozily in his pocket. What authority indeed is it that commands the waiter to share not in the gaiety? He drinks, poor fellow, hastily in isolation but still and all he drinks, keeping pace with the rest, hastening to replenish his tray, wobbling slightly.

Across the room and through the misty pall a curious spectator espies the blue and red facings, the familiar evangelical garb. Thinks he to himself, what, take a collection, seek our charitable pledges? and he sings out: 'Give us a song, old Bible-banger. Aren't you ashamed to be found in here? It's a disgrace to the cloth, I say.' And he buries his nose in his glass, conscious of having started something. Big burly Nolan offers to fight, indeed, but Harris Fudger, that soul of magnanimity, crosses the room himself and addresses the curious spectator with a great sentimentality welling within him.

'My good friend,' says he, 'come join our table and I'll show you how we evangelicals can sing.' He turns to the curious spectator's friend. 'Come all you, come and sing we will, lifting up our voices.' They arise and go with him and the men's beverage room of the Gladstone Hotel rings with a unity of purpose not readily to be achieved in these our troubled times. In vain does the floor-manager remind the crowd of the harsh regulations concerning drinking while singing; they heed him not and rightly so, say I. For what good purpose have the powers decreed that a man may not sing with his beer? A policeman looks in, senses that nothing is amiss, smiles at the floor-manager and accepts the customary beer in the seclusion of the supervisor's office while the song winds on.

Jakie Forbes, that gnome-like instigator, it is who recalls them to themselves. 'What, Harris,' he cries out, 'no news of Dasher? Nothing from the old country? What of your horse, my boy?' At this providential interpolation our hardy cornetist judges that his great moment has at length arrived, no mere captivation of an audience already half hysterical with evangelical fervour, no triple-tonguing essay of a long and exacting run on his instrument, but a song instead of money. Big money. He draws forth the crackling blue telegram from his blue and red pocket banging his glass on the table for attention while his pals bellow: 'Silence! Silence!' All the room becomes suddenly aware that there is history in their midst for Harris Fudger draws himself to his full height and, visibly transfigured before them, reads his gospel, his good news: DELIGHTED INFORM YOU DASHER PLACES FIRST DERBY YOUR TICKET WINS SIXTY THOUSAND POUNDS PLEASE CONFIRM RECEIPT MESSAGE

'How much is that in our money?' Wonders the crowd as one man.

'Nearly a hundred and fifty thousand dollars,' cries Harris, nearly fainting, stupefied with excitement and his ten ten-cent drafts. A mighty cheer goes up and two more policeman come in for their graft draft.

(In an age when liquor regulations, voting regulations, sinning regulations, rapes, catastrophes, wars, and psychoanalytical examinations of the frequency of copulation hedge the freeman round, the reader will be delighted, we anticipate, more than delighted, enraptured, he will feel a holy awe at the realization that such an increment, tainted with irregularity as it is, repels the dead paws of government. The prize is, in short, tax-free. Hurrah! Hurrah for Harris Fudger!)

'What will he do?' Queries one who stares enviously among the rest. 'How will he live? Will he, do you suppose, give up the cornet?' He is widely known as the prominent cornetist. 'How could he? The cornet is his life,' answers another. Speculation and rumour are rife; many men present will remember the scene as the most intense experience of their emotional lives. But then, ah, then!

An iciness descends upon the throng. Out of his exaltation comes Harris Fudger, out of his spasm of muscular contortion, his rictus of a triumphant grin, thinking of those dollars and his noble Dasher, that pride among horses. For a presence has come upon them all, the icy grip of retribution.

'Your habits are known,' says the bandmaster icily. 'We knew we'd find you here,' and with him, horror upon horror, is the captain.

'You know what this means, Fudger!' exclaims the captain. 'Public carousal. Oh, shameful! Shameful!'

'You left before the tutti was concluded. I told you not to leave under any circumstances,' says the bandmaster, deeply hurt. 'And I find you in this den.'

'Be at headquarters in the morning,' orders the captain. 'We'll delve into this further. Here is neither the time nor place.' He glares stoutly about him, feeling perhaps the massive resentment of the onlookers, and then, half frightened by the monolithic stares of the drinkers, the two officers turn about and leave. It is to their credit that they do not look back.

'What will they do?' wonders the crowd, bending its gaze sympathetically upon the cornetist. 'What can they do? He's got all that money. It's no skin off his nose what they do.' But he has slumped into a seat, his cohorts eyeing him with momentary discomfiture, half borne down in spite of themselves by the weight of the captain's words.

'Buck up, dear millionaire,' says Alf Pullan. 'You need never toot your horn again.'

'What can I say?' asks Harris aloud.

'What does it matter?' says Jakie Forbes.

'What indeed!' echoes Nolan Alexander.

And the waiter goes clack clack.

But the eleventh glass is lost upon poor Harris for he has been left most awesomely uncertain of his ground. 'Do you think they know about the money?' he wonders remorsefully.'I don't mind about the beer. I know what they do to beer-drinkers. But I'm too good a cornetist to lose for a matter of a beer or two.'

'Well, then,' cry his mates.

'But the beer and the sweepstakes together?'

'What then?'

'It may be too much for them. Do you suppose they know?'

Alas! Alas! Next morning all the newspapers have the story writ large in banner headlines across their grinning faces. It is a huge joke to them:

> SALVATIONIST GAMBLES AND WINS NOTED CORNETIST HOLDS SWEEP PRIZE A HUNDRED AND FIFTY THOUSAND FOR THE ARMY

There is huge consternation at headquarters; the cat is too frolicsomely out of the bag. It is a nervous captain and a jittery bandmaster who consider of the matter before their colonel, the whiles they await the coming of the backslider. The colonel has beautiful purple veins on either side his stout neck; they pulse in and bulge out to the rhythm of his agitation. Back he strides and forth across the office as the Unteroffiziers attempt an explanation.

'Drinking is bad enough,' enounces the colonel.

'Yes, sir,' they concur, submissively.

'But this – this is gambling.'

'Yes,' they admit the infection.

'On the grandest scale.'

'Well, sir,' volunteers the captain incautiously, 'the fact is that he only risked two dollars and fifty cents.'

The colonel rounds on him. 'And won a hundred and fifty thousand. It's a disgrace. A public disgrace.'

They feel it most keenly, all of them; even the secretaries and the lady volunteers at headquarters tiptoe round about with solemn visages, their bonnets, so neatly tied about the chin, wiggling up and down to the waggling of their busy tongues. Bob-bob-bob go the bonnets above the secretarial desks, the anteroom seems alive with them; it is like a field of red and blue flowers stilled all at once by the cessation of the breeze as the poor hundredthousandaire makes his reluctant entry, his eyes red-rimmed by his close study of the affair. He is ushered into the colonel's office by a bobbing bonnet. The door slams.

Like the dead march from *Saul* the next minutes drag funereally along as the clustered bonnets in the anteroom turn like sunflowers more and more intensely towards the colonel's heavy door. No sound comes: there is nothing for what seems like hours together. The bobbing little heads and tongues come gradually to horrified rest as at first there are murmurs from within the monstrous cave and then clear voices and at length, climactically, shouting, thumping and banging, most emphatic point-making, threats, brow-beatings and a feeble defence.

'You are a very lucky cornet-player,' hurls the colonel. 'Lucky that we don't snip off your buttons publicly.'

'You're lucky we don't take back your presentation cornet,' puts in the bandmaster, aside.

'It's my cornet,' says Fudger blearily. 'It's got my name engraved on it.'

'But who presented it to you?'

'It was for years of faithful service.'

'Yes. But what have you done for us lately?' asks the captain, thinking of a joke which he has heard for the first time on television, the night before.

'Look what you've done!'

'Only look!'

'Just look!'

'The publicity!!'

'I was always brought up to believe,' says Fudger hopefully, 'that it doesn't matter what they say about you as long as they spell your name right.' For some reason this angers them still further.

'You're being insolent, you ... you instrumentalist,' says the colonel, groping for words. Poor colonel, his feet hurt and he is old and doesn't know what to make of it all. 'I'm sorry, Fudger, deeply sorry, but you'll have to go.'

'Go?'

'Go! Get out. Leave us. You're a public embarrassment to the organization.'

'But but but, I can't go. Where would I go? I was brought up in the army. I'm an army baby, trained to be an army musician from birth. I can't play any other type of music.'

'Drinking, gambling, tainted money.'

'I was going to give you half.'

'Tainted, I say!'

'A tainted seventy-five thousand dollars.'

The colonel and the captain and the bandmaster exchange glances; they do not know what to make of this effrontery. Money, indeed, forsooth, money! The colonel manages to pull himself together to repeat his sentence: 'We'll spare your feelings. We won't have a public ceremony of expulsion. But you're no longer with us, do you hear? If you pass yourself off as one of us in public, we'll sue you. Please leave.' Still goggling, unable to comprehend this dreadful dismissal, poor Fudger is led, not unkindly, to the door where he takes his dismal way away.

Of some similar heroes it is recorded that they cried all the way to the bank, with an ironic implication that their tears were not deeply felt from their toes upwards. Of Fudger, the irony would be inaccurate. Cry all the way to the bank he did, poor fellow, but he felt it deeply. He would consult his bankers, he told himself, and though he were an outcast upon the face of the city, there might still be a kind of life in him.

His new-found friends, the bankers, received him kindly. Yes, they had been in communication with the sweepstakes authority. Yes, there was a hundred and fifty thousand lying to his credit on deposit. They handed him his cheque-book, his pass-book, a cigar, and several stock-prospectuses. He was one of them, they implied. They stood ready to lay out his money for him at its maximum growth potential in carefully selected common stocks. He might expect a steady five-percent yield and capital gains as well. He need never lift a hand. They thought it over and gave him another cigar. He asked for ready money. They told him not to dip into capital and gave him a thousand in cash, telling him that his income would be credited to him quarterly. He left in some bewilderment.

When he went, as of course he must, to the men's beverage room of the Gladstone Hotel, everything seemed changed. He greeted Jakie Forbes and Alf Pullan, waving a clutch of fifty-dollar bills.

'Good day, Mr Fudger,' they said obsequiously. 'How do you do, sir.'

So he went to a table by himself and had a bottle of beer, not a glass. He had never felt so wealthy.

The Fable of the Ant and the Grasshopper

With quite the deepest of bows to the Master – *James Thurber*

IN THE SUMMER every green leaf was ripe for tearing; the grasses too were long, bending rhythmically as the soft breeze swept across them. In the forest of grasses and leaves, there dwelt a colony of insects: ants, grasshoppers, and even some slugs, for this was a liberal-minded colony which had been founded by agrarian progressives in the eighties. Originally utopian-communist in conception and design, the little colony had through the years gradually evolved a moderate modern capitalism. But even yet the ambitious entrepreneurs – most of them ants – lived on easy friendly terms with their consumption-oriented neighbours the grasshoppers. The slugs constituted an anonymous proletariat.

In this arboreal paradise of organic matter lived a certain grasshopper whom I shall call Dalton Grasshopper III. Dalton was a descendant of one of the original settlers, an aristocratic black sheep who had emigrated to the infant colony from beyond the pond, under a cloud. Not a great cloud, you must understand, but still there had descended to the third generation a faint trace of glamorous shiftlessness.

Dalton Grasshopper III was handsome, lithe, a bit of a bounder, one might think, but his charm was undeniable. He spoke in a pleasant clipped old-country accent, had been to the best prep schools, and possessed many graceful accomplishments such as were sure to beguile the ladies. Sometimes he wore spats and often he was to be seen in the early evening perched on the very extremity of a tall blade of grass swinging athletically to and fro as he plunked the strings of an old guitar. At these times he was the cynosure of all eyes, the pampered darling of a way of life whose days seemed numbered. 'Hotcha!' he would sing, as he plunked a chord or two. 'Hotcha!'

Every day, at the base of the tall grasses where the heat was most oppressive, the ants scurried hither and thither conducting their involved affairs. Rumours circulated feverishly in the sand beneath the grass, along the winding roots, of this or that financial coup, of the formation of some titanic cartel – usually in sugar – or of the collapse of a great industrial empire, or possibly of the pyramiding of a holding company.

When such rumours were bandied about, the name certain to appear in the context was that of an ant whom I shall have to protect, as I have protected Dalton Grasshopper III, under the cloak of a pseudonym; let us call this industrious fellow Oscar Ant. Oscar was not the third of any line of succession, nor the second. He was a hard-bitten infighter who had climbed from the depths of the anthill to a commanding position above ground relying not upon his ancestry or upon his looks, which were by no means taking, but upon sheer native cunning, foresight, and financial genius. Oscar Ant voted the straight Conservative ticket and he hated Dalton Grasshopper III with something like a pure philosophical ardour.

What was wealth, what the use of command, where were to be found the delights of paper empire, if one remained a groundling, a crawler upon anthills, an irredeemably middle-class dealer in stocks and shares, a haunter of the marts of commerce? Thus it was that Oscar Ant brooded, when he allowed himself leisure to consider such things. Where was he going? He had ambitions to found a line, to hand his name imperially down to later generations. He bought pictures and supported ballet dancers but it did him no good. He extended his chain of aphids and thought of branching out, of extending his hegemony to a neighbouring anthill, of finally dominating the entire colony. A convenient marriage to Amanda Ant, heiress to a vast fortune, beckoned to him; but despite her undeniable good sense Amanda was a dowdy middle-aged ant who had no style. And so Oscar sat in his suburban ranch-house and brooded and made plans. Which was better, he wondered, to be the first of a line or the last?

Above him in the August night he could hear Dalton's guitar and an occasional chord or two. 'Give a man a horse he can ride!' sang Dalton energetically.

Of all the young ladies in the colony there can be no doubt that Georgia Grasshopper had the highest style, the brightest polish, the never-to-be-counterfeited glitter, the real thing. She flouted convention, danced all night by the light of the moon, rose late in the afternoon, captivated ants and grasshoppers alike. She was a blithesome, lissome lass, a long tall beauty of aristocratic mien. Oscar adored her but she knew him not; she hung adoringly upon the negligent arm of Dalton Grasshopper III at the polo matches, the theatre, in his convertible. They were a pair of whom Housman might have sung if he'd been a grasshopper.

All that golden summer Oscar Ant dug himself into his work, studying balance sheets, amassing wealth, waiting and pondering what must surely come. He was waiting for winter, a downturn in the business cycle, a shrinkage in fixed inherited income, for he realized cannily that his rival's assets yielded income only as the market flourished. When production should fall off, when snow should blanket the hard frosty ground, where would the scion of inheritance be? Aha! thought Oscar. Aha! Had he possessed a moustache he'd have twirled it.

Autumn came and the edges of the leaves grew brown. The grasses withered and grew brittle; there was no swinging on them now. The grasshoppers returned to earth and Dalton ceased singing in public, spending his time instead in cozy bars or at his club buying drinks for his friends. You had to say this for Dalton: he was good when he had it. Once in a while he'd go downtown, inspect the big board, and realize in a vague way that his holdings weren't doing terribly well. His quarterly cheques shrank in size; the leaves grew sere and began to fall; there was no more grass now.

On these ill-informed and sloppily conducted sallies into the world of finance, Dalton often passed Oscar on the street. He only knew the other insect by sight and, vaguely, by reputation, but he was always cordial, never administering a snub. 'Ah there, Ant!' he might say, swinging his cane. 'We must get together for lunch,' and off he'd debonairly go.

Behind him, caught flat-footed on the hard pavement, thinking of Georgia, Oscar came closer and closer to the boiling-point.

His lamp burned late into the night now, as autumn wore

along; he often sat up till two or three comparing market-reports, buying this block of stock and unloading that. He was more like a spider than an ant these days and the strain was telling on him. But ever more surely he projected his influence over the entire financial structure of the colony; and ever more vividly could he foresee the ruin of his rival. Large supplies of capital were what was needed in this kind of manoeuvring and Dalton had no superfluous capital to risk. The situation grew more and more liquid; income yield shrank apace. One morning, waking in the grey dawn after falling asleep over his documents at 3:00 a.m., Oscar saw that a light snow had fallen, that the ground was frozen underfoot. Winter had set in early and it was a long time till spring.

On the very next night was held the most splendid social occasion of the season – the Ant-Grasshopper Cotillion Ball – a magnificent masquerade given each season in commemoration of the liberal live-and-let-live principles of the founding fathers. Never much of a party-goer, Oscar hesitated to attend but this year he was on the committee for the first time, in recognition of his growing importance to the community. He knew that he would see Georgia and Dalton but he had to be there. He rented the costume of a dashing gaucho – a range-rider of the pampas – and feeling dreadfully out of place arrived at the ball just in time to see Dalton, magnificently gotten up as Heliogabalus, lead Georgia, a Nubian princess, forth at the head of the first quadrille.

Oh, it was hell for Oscar Ant! He sat on the platform trying to ignore the gabble of the dowagers but once he heard one of them say: 'Yes, yes. An immediate engagement. And aren't they such a sweet couple.' As soon as he decently could he fled into the night.

Next morning he summoned his lieutenants and outlined his plans for an immense coup, giving directions swiftly and consulting the ticker continually. He knew that Dalton's income was chiefly derived from holdings in Inter-Colonial Grass and Leaf; he aimed to drive Inter-Colonial through the floor, to reduce its quotation to nothing. Only utter destruction would satisfy him. By the end of that day, with ticker running five hours behind, he had precipitated a panic and

Inter-Colonial shares were worthless. The company's president, an elderly grey-headed grasshopper, went home and put a bullet through his brain. The vice-president leaped from his own penthouse. There would be no more income, no more serenades, no plunking of guitars, no dazzling nuptials. Dalton was through.

Sitting cozily at home after his frugal dinner, under the first flakes of a two-day blizzard, Oscar reviewed his situation and found it good. He was master of the colony; nothing could stand out against him; the future was limitless, entrancing. He was far sunk in fantastic reverie when there came a knock at the door. He had given the staff a night off so he answered it himself. Framed in the doorway, a bizarre figure in the hard night light, was Dalton Grasshopper III.

'What do you want?' asked Oscar brusquely, concealing a nameless terror which gripped his heart.

'Bread,' said the other. 'No one will honour my credit-cards. I've had nothing to eat all day.' His voice cracked. 'Why do you hate me so?' he cried. 'I've never done you any harm.'

'You exist,' snarled Oscar. 'That's enough.'

'For God's sake,' said Dalton. 'I am hungry. I need help.'

Oscar laughed. 'When you were playing around all summer annoying the rest of us with your singing, I was working and planning. You see the result.'

'Very well,' said Dalton with a queer dignity. 'I won't beg,' and he turned away.

'Effete!' jeered Oscar. 'Effete! Ask your friends for help, your friends in the clubs and bars.' But Dalton was already out of hearing, striding defiantly along, not quite done yet. No sir, he told himself, I'm not beaten yet. The blood of generations of grasshoppers raced hotly in his veins. And though he was dizzy from hunger he managed to reach his university club. There, licking their wounds, were seven other grasshoppers larger than himself, who had suffered much from Oscar Ant that day. He rallied them, did Dalton, he put life and heart in them and their resentment burned brighter. Putting on their hats and coats they retraced the way to Oscar's comfortable suburban residence. When they arrived they pounded lustily on the door and Oscar, like a sucker, answered them.

They dragged him outside and knocked him down, kicking him. They beat the hell out of him, in fact, and left him insensible and bloody on the snowy ground. The snow was fully a blizzard now, falling in thick stiff flakes. Then the eight grasshoppers went inside, slamming the door.

It was some time before the freezing air brought Oscar to his senses for he had been badly hurt. When he revived, he dragged himself slowly, with an enormous effort, some fifteen feet to the picture window. It was obscured with a misty haze but inside he could hear singing, and the sound of bottles being opened.

The beating and the effort had been too much for him and, with a sigh which went unheard by the universe, he released his grasp on the window-sill and slid back to the ground. Soon, the snow covered him up.

THE MORAL: Never oppress the shiftless and the idle; they may have powerful friends.

I'm Not Desperate!

'ALLUSIVE WITTY TALK,' Tony said, 'witty allusive talk. Here we are, you and me, sitting in this dungeon enjoying our oblique elliptical witty allusive talk.' He kept letting his eyes go out of focus.

'It's not so bad,' I said.

'You're damned right it's not so bad,' he said, 'we've both been in the army and now that's over. We don't have to worry about that any more.'

'It was a waste of time,' I said.

'Sure it was,' he said, 'they abused our gifts. They made us be typists instead of teachers but that's all over now. We've done it, and besides,' he gave me a threatening look, 'a man ought to serve his country.'

'Ought?' I said, underlining it, 'OUGHT?'

'Sure he ought. It's a dignified and honourable thing to do.' He rolled his eyes at me.

'Where did you get this morals kick?' I asked. Actually, I knew pretty well what he'd say.

He put down his glass and signalled to the waiter who'd thrown us out the night before. I think, one of these days, we're going to be cut off by the manager for singing. The waiter came, all the same.

'My round,' I said.

'A decent thing, an honourable thing,' he said, as though he had a grievance, 'you pay for one round, I pay for the next, and we don't argue about the right and wrong of it. We know the rules.'

'Two!' I said. The waiter brought two draft beers.

'What are you grinning at?' he said. Tony, that is.

'I don't know,' I said, 'we're not so very moral.'

'Sure we are,' he said, 'we're served our country. I don't know why that sounds so funny.'

'It isn't funny,' I said, 'it lasted two years and now we're too old to date the undergraduate women.'

'That's no loss.'

'No.'

'Anyway, we're mature. We've been sobered by the experience. We have literary minds, we're men of letters. That's dignified, isn't it? The American man of letters, graceful and urbane, pottering amongst his books and his flowers.'

'Like old Berenson,' I said.

'Just so,' he said. He's full of these literary coinages, 'just so. An essay here, a travel book there, perhaps an appreciation of the poetry of Mark Van Doren.'

'Or possibly Wallace Stevens.'

'No,' he said, 'you don't see the joke. Anyway, Wallace Stevens was too good. I revere Wallace Stevens, if I were old enough I'd have contributed a graceful and urbane essay to the Stevens issue of some quarterly. "Homage to Wallace Stevens." *You* know.'

'Drink your beer!'

'Are you watching that waiter?'

'Certainly I am. You owe me a round.'

'Oh,' he said sadly, 'you shouldn't have mentioned that.'

'I can't help it,' I said, 'I'm insecure about money. I always have been.'

'That's a disfigurement.'

'I know,' I said, 'but there are lots worse.'

'One should do nothing mean,' he said. He was just beginning to feel the beer. I noticed that he finished this glass in a hurry. That's always a sign, with Tony. He drinks them faster and faster and finally gets quite drunk, but I've never seen him *drunk*, if you know what I mean. 'One should affirm the possibility of the good, the dutiful life, I affirm it,' he said. 'I affirm the meaning of humanly created values.'

'Sure,' I said, 'pay!'

'Oh,' he said, looking up at the waiter mistrustfully, 'thirty cents for the beer and ten for you.' Then he squinted at me. 'I see where this Mauriac has written a book.'

'He's written forty books,' I said, 'for Christ's sake.'

'That's the other one you're thinking of, the father,' he said, 'the one with the sense of sin.'

'Exactly,' I said, 'for Christ's sake,' I was making a joke.

'For Christ's sake, and his own, and his publisher's.'

'That's right.'

'Don't joke about it,' he said, 'there are all these different sources of morals.'

'All right,' I said, 'I'm sorry.'

'I forgive you,' he said, 'it's a complicated, bitter, ironic post-Christian joke, typical of the post-Christian intellectual. Anyway, I was referring to the other Mauriac, the young one, Mauriac's son.'

'Claude.'

'*The Ferocious Tiger*,' he said, 'by Claude Ball. That's a joke I heard in the seventh grade.'

'It doesn't stand up.'

'There are a lot of those,' he said. '*The Splash in the Pond* by Aileen Dover.'

'All right, all right, what about Mauriac?' He was starting to indulge his infantilism.

'It's all about the younger French novelist,' he said, 'the generation under thirty, "*dans l'an trentième de mon âge*," the writers you haven't heard of yet.'

'Neither have you,' I said. After all, who has?

'They're just about your age, and my God, what bores!' he said, 'I'm getting damned sick of hearing about the younger French novelists. Mauriac seems to take them seriously.'

'The French take all their writers seriously, especially the young ones. They can't help it. Look at that nine-year-old poet.'

'Poetess.'

'Yes. And Sagan, my God! If Sagan was a nice American kid who'd done a book called *Teenage Madness,* who'd give her a second thought?'

'She ought to be spanked,' he said, 'she's such a dreary thing.' He's always hated that sort of nine-days' wonder. Tony thinks nobody under thirty knows enough to write a book. He's twenty-seven himself. I'm twenty-eight. 'Who cares what the younger French writers think?' he said.

'The people who read the *Times Book Review*.'

'Sure,' he said, 'and then they get the idea, in Larchmont or somewhere, that the younger French novelists have something deeply significant to say.'

'It's all been said before. It's nothing new,' I said.

'Value nihilism,' he said disgustedly, 'I wouldn't mind if it weren't so silly. A nation of barbarians civilized by the conscription.'

'Who said that?'

'I don't know. Maybe Poincaré. I don't know. But it's true. They act as though they were the first people in the history of the world to go on living after a disaster.'

'They aren't,' I said. I know all about disasters, having witnessed two or three.

'Mauriac quotes one of them,' he said ferociously, 'to this effect: "Our only affirmation is that we affirm nothing for there can be nothing to affirm. He is damned and a liar who dares affirm anything. There is only negation and nothing means anything, negation is what is. The truly mortal sin is the affirmation.' And so on, and on, the same old inconsistent dreary round. What annoys me about it, is that it flies in the face of the given facts of morals.'

'There are no facts in morals.'

He gave me a disgusted look. 'Of course there are,' he said, 'and don't pretend that you don't know what I'm talking about. Morals exist factually, and they can be described. They're known to exist.'

'That doesn't mean that they appear in truth-conferring sentences,' I said, to kid him along. We'd had the same argument several times before and I wanted to see if he had thought of anything new. He worries a question like this like a dog with a smelly old bone. He can't bear to let such a question drop. The first time I saw him after we got out of the army, he took up the conversation in the exact place where we'd left it two years before. This doesn't imply, mind you, that he ever comes up with any answers.

'Listen,' he said impatiently, leaning forward in his chair and sticking his elbow in a pool of beer on the table. 'I'm not trying to legislate a particular scheme of morals. All I'm saying is that morals and conduct unquestionably are the case, that is, they exist. We find no human person, who possesses the customary human powers, who does not conduct himself. Conduct is inevitable.'

'So what?'

He looked at the leather patch on his elbow; it was wet and the leather smelled bad, from the beer. 'Get the next one,' he said, 'I'm going to the men's room.' He got up, quite steady on his feet, and marched off down the aisle. I sat looking after him thinking that nothing would come of the argument, though I had to admire his point of view – he's the only person I know who has the courage to be provincial. He has no Picasso reproduction in his room and he once bought a drawing from a painter we sometimes drink with. He paid fifteen dollars for it and had it framed, with glass. I was glad to hear him damn the younger French novelists because they don't carry much weight, after all, and we only defer to them because they speak such good French.

I must have met a couple of hundred European students, in my time, and as many imported professors, and they all act as though they're God's gift to American learning because they speak four languages including their own. I've had a lot of fun pointing out that the only reason they can all speak four languages is that the countries are so small. You go for a pleasant Sunday afternoon drive – and all of a sudden you're in some other country.

This annoys them. Then I always point out that French, Spanish, Italian, Latin, German, English, the Scandinavian tongues, oh, and I forgot Dutch, are only dialects anyway, and that any fool should be able to read them all at sight, and speak them after three months' residence. I'm sick of being browbeaten by intellectual imperialists, which is what they are. Tony agrees with me.

He came back from the men's room looking pleased with himself.

'Stebbins is in there,' he said, 'being sick. He gave me the two dollars.'

'Oh, good! How much have you got altogether?'

'Five seventy-five.'

'I've got nearly five,' I said, 'and I just paid for a round.'

He looked at the full glass on the table thirstily. 'I feel great,' he said, 'and we've got nearly ten dollars. I'll tell you what we'll do. We'll spend a dollar fifty each for supper, no more. That'll leave us seven dollars for tonight. If we drink drafts that's, let's see, that's fifteen into six hundred – I'm allowing a dollar for the waiter,' he said generously, 'that's forty glasses or a total of twenty apiece. 'We'll never get through that.'

'God!' I said, 'I hope not.'

'You see?' he said, excitedly.

'See what?'

'You swore. You said "God!" That's an oath.'

'Now look,' I said, 'don't carry this too far.'

'I'm not criticizing you,' he said, 'I'm just showing that you involuntarily invoked a source of morality. Men do this instinctively.' You see? He won't let an idea go. 'Everyone justifies his wishes and his acts by referring them to sanctions. Men conduct themselves. That may even be tautological. It may even be the case that to be a man you've got to be moral. In fact, I think it is the case. Man is a value-secreting animal and the only one there is.'

'You can't prove it.'

'Yes, you can,' he said excitedly, 'with the identical weapon that's for so long been used to deny it, the certainty, statistically speaking, that a probability is as certain as the statistical calculation asserts it to be.'

'Statistics are mumbo-jumbo,' I said, 'everybody knows that.'

'Whether with them or without them,' he said, 'we're forced to concede the existence of conduct. All men conduct themselves. Physicists and statisticians have values and act on them *before* they can do physics or statistics. Morality creates the possibility of science. Conduct is logically prior to science, and a moral intuition of the right and the good precedes all quantitative calculi.'

'So?'

'All sciences of numbers are based on morals because unity is fundamentally a moral concept. It is *absolutely better* to be one, than to be two or more.'

'Where are we going to eat?' I asked. It was getting close to closing time.

'Eat!' he said. 'Eat. That's all you ever think about.'

'There's the other thing,' I said.

'What other thing?' he was getting slower on the uptake.

'Sex.'

'I count that with eating. It's all the same. It's all appetite.'

'There's nothing wrong with appetite.'

'Of course not,' he said generously. He tries to see all sides of any question. 'Look at our appetite for beer! Nevertheless, we can control our appetites morally.'

'We can?'

'Damn right. We don't have to have a good time to drink.'

'True.'

'Alcohol is no crutch in our lives.'

'No.'

'We've got it under control. We don't spend all our time in little bars. We're responsible members of society.'

'We'd better order,' I said.

'All right,' he said. Stebbins came out of the men's room and up the aisle, looking green. He stopped beside our table. If there's one thing I hate when I'm drinking beer, it's table-hoppers.

'I thought you were sitting in the other room,' Tony said.

'Janice got sick and went home,' Stebbins said. He was waiting for us to ask him to sit down. We weren't under any obligation to ask him and I was glad to see that Tony felt this.

'I need the two dollars back,' said Stebbins. He looked at Tony impatiently.

'I need it,' Tony said. 'I'm going drinking tonight.'

'You lent it to me before.'

'That doesn't mean I have to lend it to you again.'

'Come on!'

'No,' Tony said. 'I don't have to be a good fellow all the time. I'm not running for any popularity contest.'

Stebbins looked at me and I looked right back at him. 'It's useless to ask you,' he said.

'That's right,' I told him. He lurched off up the aisle and I saw him stop beside somebody else.

'It's a matter of principle,' said Tony. 'I want that money for myself, as it happens. I don't always have to sacrifice my own interests to those of others, especially when I don't like them.'

'Stebbins isn't much,' I said.

'He thinks history is a social science,' Tony said. 'Whoever heard of a social science with a Muse? Clio, the Muse of history!'

'I wonder what the Muse of time and motion study is?'

'Or clinical psychology, or the marginal utility theory.'

'Yeah,' I said. 'Mumbo-Jumbo, the Muse of statistics!'

Tony guffawed. 'Stebbins has no Muse,' he said. 'I don't know why I lent him the two dollars in the first place.' The waiter brought another round and we ordered our last before dinner; we were really hurling them down.

'I don't think one is obliged to be nice to everybody, at all times,' Tony said uneasily. He was still worrying about Stebbins.

'The hell with him,' I said. 'You're a good man, Tony.'

'I am,' he said, very intensely, which is another sign. I was glad we were leaving before he began to sing. I don't know why I always sing with him. It's caused me a lot of trouble here and there.

'I make very little money,' he said. 'I sacrifice my immediate interests for a distant purpose. That takes discipline.'

'It does,' I said, to placate him.

'Mauriac says the younger French novelists are desperate. He says they reject all values.'

'They can't do that.'

'No,' he said, 'they can't do that.' He looked for a minute as if he were going to slump over the table.

'Don't go to sleep,' I said.

He stuck his head straight up on his shoulders and stared at me. 'I have hope!' he said loudly. 'I'm not desperate, because I have hope!'

'What in?'

'I don't know,' he said, 'I'm honourable. I try never to do anything willingly that I think is wrong. I'm virtuous.' He looked embarrassed. 'That sounds crazy, doesn't it?'

'I don't know,' I said, 'it sounds like a lot of things.'

'I make a hundred and sixty dollars a month from a teaching assistantship,' he said, 'and I'm not a charge on anybody. I try always to tell the truth.'

'You're a good man,' I said. I knew that's what he wanted to hear. The waiter brought the last round before they closed for the dinner hour.

'I have faith and hope!!' he said.

'Well,' I said, 'that's two of them.'

'Everybody has morals,' he said, 'if they're here at all.'

'We're certainly here,' I said, 'and this is certainly good beer. I mean *morally* good. Isn't it?'

Friends and Relations

MILLICENT HOLMAN wept incoherently, self-indulgently and without real sorrow, sitting in the bathtub splashing water on her pretty face and, as always, refusing to think through a matter which genuinely puzzled her. She left such exercises to her husband. Faced with a puzzle or a mystery, especially if other people were involved, she preferred simply to stare at it with her pretty pout, hoping that it would solve itself or disappear.

'I'm hopeless, I know,' she wailed without meaning it. She was as by no means hopeless; she was very young-looking, had a little money inherited from a great-aunt, and had stayed married, and in fact meant to go on staying married.

'I can't understand mother at all,' she moaned, her voice muffled by bubbles. She fished around for the soap, seized it, and began to scrub her back and shoulders energetically.

'Do me lower down!' she commanded her husband, who was shaving.

James Holman put down his razor with an imperceptible sigh, twisted his face into a grimace at the mirror, and bending began to soap his wife's back. He felt the soap bump over her vertebrae with a see-saw motion.

'There's no need to cry,' he said hopefully. 'She'll come another time.' He admired his mother-in-law, the redoubtable Mrs Lawson Bird, genuinely and extravagantly, and never quite knew what she was up to.

'I'm her only daughter,' wept Millicent, 'and I love her dearly. And she refuses to come and see us.'

'She doesn't refuse to see us,' said James calmly, 'she'll come and see us, all right. She simply has other things to think about.'

'She shouldn't have other things to think about,' said Millicent pettishly, quite aware of her tone and position. 'She hasn't been to see us in over a year. She hasn't seen the baby walk or talk.' She rinsed herself and stood up, a column of pearly pink marble, a Venus of the bathtub, Botticellian.

Her husband regarded her admiringly, in spite of himself.

'She must have three hundred pictures of Jassy,' he said, turning to finish his interrupted shave. Millicent tossed her head, threw on her housecoat and sidled past him into their bedroom. He was obliged to wipe the steam off the shaving mirror a second time. Millicent habitually filled the tub to the brim with steaming hot water.

'Pictures aren't the same,' he heard her complain from the bedroom, 'and I wonder what she's doing in Montreal.'

He began to laugh cheerfully; he was looking forward to their evening out. 'I'm sure I know,' he said lewdly.

Millicent was as usual scandalized by the hint.

When Millicent Holman's father, Dr Lawson Bird, had died three years before, he had been the best-known dentist in Eastern Ontario, and among the best technically. He had not been trained as a specialist but had acquired a very considerable proficiency in oral surgery over the years, and had cases referred to him from a hundred miles away. But much more than his professional attainments, which were quite real and valuable, his hobbies and activities had made him widely known.

He had, for example, played semi-pro hockey every winter until he was past forty and it was widely rumoured that as a younger man he had turned down professional offers and might have played for the Maple Leafs if his career hadn't intervened. This was not strictly true. He had never been a fast enough skater to be a professional but he played excellent Senior-B hockey with locally sponsored teams. He was a stocky rough defenceman, known on the sports pages of many small eastern Ontario weeklies as 'the denting dentist' or 'the extracter' in reference to his habit of scoring crucial last period goals.

He had founded the Stoverville camera club and was an excellent amateur photographer who had sold news and candid shots to the Toronto papers. He owned two boats, a launch for trolling and a one-design sloop which he raced, and in the summer was on the Saint Lawrence at every moment that could be spared from his extensive practice. He belonged to an exclusive hunting lodge owned by several rich friends of his in Stoverville, which is a town with money in it. He played a fair game of golf, collected records – his taste running as high as Brahms – and was in short a man of solid professional worth and many graceful and attractive personal accomplishments. When he was alive, the people who came to the Birds' home were his friends or his relatives – he belonged to an enormous and enormously ramified old Stoverville family.

Mrs Bird seemed to prefer to stay in the background. Her husband was so popular, so widely known, so genuinely loved and admired, and her daughter – their only child – such a vivid gay girl, that the Birds' friends and relations hardly remembered that Mrs Bird was around the house at all, except of course, at mealtime.

She had been trained as a nurse before her marriage and spent long hours nursing the dozen elderly invalids who composed the senior stratum of Dr Bird's family connection, suffering many disappointments and rebuffs in this charitable and kindly activity. These old people were hard – immensely hard – to please. Some of them were absolute monsters of senile rancour; she was accused regularly of theft, sometimes of intrigue, and it was made plain to her that she was only a Bird by marriage.

One ancient aunt of Dr Bird's after Mrs Bird had spent ten years in caring for her during her decline, actually, specifically and by name, cut her out of her will, charging that she was an unworthy wife for Dr Lawson.

Mrs Bird said nothing to this; she knew what the old and sick can imagine as they lie in bed with nothing to do but stoke the fires of their resentment. She knew that she had been kindness itself to the old aunt.

She didn't let herself be daunted; everyone in the family must know that what Aunt Sarah asserted was false, or if they didn't they certainly should have. The one great reward that Mrs Bird looked for was the opportunity to take care of Lawson, really at last to be able to do something for him, if his health should fail before hers.

But she was denied the chance. Three years ago Dr Bird suffered a coronary attack while trolling on the river. By the time his companion could get him ashore he was beyond help. He died during the night in the Stoverville General, quite literally mourned by everyone who had known him.

He had served as the chairman of the board of education for

several years and the Stoverville schools were closed on the day following his death and on the following Monday, the day of the funeral.

He was only fifty-four years old and had just begun to earn more than he spent, which was a lot. He had always lived on a large scale, had been a free and generous spender, and the cost of his multitudinous hobbies and interests had been very great. He had for example just bought an enormous outboard motor, paid cash for it and never used it. When it finally came to be sold, it brought Mrs Bird about one-fifth what the doctor had paid for it. It was, by this time, a last year's model, and it was hard to find a buyer.

It became evident very speedily that Ruthie, as Mrs Bird was known in the family, was going to be left with very little. When the final balance came to be set, what was left was a few thousand in cash and the value of the outstanding accounts at the office. Mrs Bird felt no surprise or disappointment on the score of her inheritance. She had known vaguely that her husband's insurance programme was not in satisfactory shape. He had alluded to it once or twice in passing, saying that he had bought his insurance in the late thirties, and that while it had seemed like enough at the time, it certainly wasn't these days. He had been meaning to do something about it but had gone along putting it off.

It was a stroke of good fortune that Millicent's wedding had taken place a few months before the doctor's death instead of afterwards. It had cost him thousands, money which came from current income and from the sale of a piece of riverfront property he had been hanging on to for years; he had intended to build a combination boathouse, cottage, and hunting lodge on it. But he gladly spent the money on the wedding instead. After the ceremony James and Millicent had moved to the United States to live and they were not in Stoverville when the doctor died.

When they heard, in the middle of the night, they were surprised and shocked. In the morning they started up from Connecticut by car, arriving in time to attend the beginnings of the solemn family council which began the evening after Dr Lawson died and continued at intervals for over a year. All were perplexed at 'poor Ruthie's' situation, and they grew more perplexed and reluctant to make any positive cash commitments as the facts concerning the doctor's estate grew clearer.

'Of course you can come and live with me, Ruthie,' said old Aunt Cleila, her eyes moist and glittering, 'Lawson would want you to.'

'No, I don't believe I will,' said Mrs Bird positively, with an unfamiliar briskness. The old aunts and uncles were a trifle taken aback at her brusquerie. They had been so used to her habitual self-effacement that it came as a surprise to them to see her make a choice of her own.

She told her son-in-law much later that Aunt Cleila had discharged her housemaid as soon as she heard about Lawson, meaning to have 'poor Ruthie' supply the gap.

'What do they think I am?' she asked James, strictly privately, 'do they imagine that I don't know what a housemaid gets paid these days?'

James grinned. 'I won't invite you to Hartford,' he said. 'I don't want you thinking such things about us.'

'Gracious,' she said, with the faintest touch of asperity, 'I know I can come to you at any time, James.' She smiled at him kindly, almost, he suspected, patronizingly. 'You must lead a pretty quiet life these days,' she hazarded.

'We do,' he assented, wondering what she was really thinking.

The aunts and uncles, and Dr Bird's cousins and connections, who between them dominated Stoverville society – for there is 'society' even in Stoverville – were aghast at Ruthie's cavalier dismissal of Aunt Cleila's offer. They decided amongst themselves that she must be holding out for something more comfortable. She had, they estimated, enough money to live on for about two years. When that was exhausted her independence would be much reduced. They could hardly contain themselves for so long.

'Come to us and care for the children. We'll pay you a small honorarium and you'll have your nights free,' said Cousin Roger, the Cadillac dealer.

'Oh, Roger, don't you see,' she smiled inflexibly, 'it's been fifteen years since I had anything to do with young children.'

Cousin Roger, who knew a thing or two about the management of staff, domestic and business, felt that he had met his match.

Finally Uncle Maurice came to see her one night, in all the weight of his seniority as the oldest male member of the family. He had always liked Ruthie, and found her pale and uninteresting, though a good nurse. He was at this time mayor of Stoverville.

'Now, look here, Ruthie,' he told her kindly, 'you won't be able to stay in this house much longer. After all, it doesn't belong to you.'

It was true. It belonged to some Toronto cousins who meant to spend their retirement in Stoverville; they had let Dr Lawson have it for a nominal rent while he lived. Now their retirement was approaching and they wanted the house.

'Grover and Pauline will be moving down here this summer,' said the mayor. 'You don't want to be in their way when they come.'

'Of course not, Uncle Maurice,' said Ruthie with alacrity. The old man felt encouraged, and went on.

'I'm prepared to find you a good job downtown,' he said. 'I heard today that there's an opening for a saleslady in the Mode Shoppe.'

'I don't think I'd like waiting on the people in Stoverville,' said Mrs Bird with a faint smile.

It was on the tip of Uncle Maurice's tongue to tell her that she had no choice; but something in her manner warned him and he held his peace.

'Won't you tell me,' he said at length, in great puzzlement, 'what you think you'd like to do?'

'Of course, ' she said pleasantly and with a funny composure. 'I'd like to find something that will get me out of Stoverville for a while.'

'Do you fancy anything in particular?' asked Uncle Maurice dryly. He had a glimmer of what was going through her head.

'Why, yes,' she said, 'I believe I'll have a try at real estate.'

'Real estate?'

'Yes.'

'I see,' he said in amazement. 'Well ... if I can help you in any way, Ruthie, I hope you'll let me know.' He was really a nice old fellow, was Uncle Maurice.

'Perhaps you can swing some business my way,' said Mrs Bird cheerfully, as she showed him to the door.

Without waiting for the news of her decision to spread around town, Mrs Bird placed the accounts receivable from the dental practice in the hands of a collection agency (an act which infuriated a great many of the late doctor's clients) took what cash she had with her and left for Toronto without saying goodbye to anyone. She caught on as a trainee with a big-time real estate broker, and for nine months made no sales although she trailed hundreds of clients through development houses in the far-ranging Toronto suburbs. She wrote to James and Millicent now and then, recounting her hilarious adventures and misadventures. A fifty-five-year-old Hungarian with extensive rooming-house properties was pursuing her (she was herself a year or two under fifty) escorting her to Czardas Café for the two-dollar goulash dinner. He proposed marriage and the investment of her accounts receivable in more rooming houses for more immigrants. He also had a project for a Hungarian daily which he hoped she might back.

The manager of the branch office was swiping her clients as soon as she got them interested in anything, and closing with them.

'I don't mind that,' she wrote, 'because he knows I can turn him in to the real estate board any time, so he gives me extra training. I didn't expect to make any money while I'm learning the tricks; it's like an apprenticeship. Anyway, it shows that I can soften a prospect up for the kill pretty well.'

When James Holman read this, he laughed immoderately, in a way that made his wife very angry.

'I don't know what you're laughing at,' Millicent said in the tones of extreme vexation, 'that horrible man's simply taking advantage of her.'

'Sure he is,' said James, laughing, 'and she knows it. She's terribly sharp. She knows they wouldn't dream of paying her while she's learning the business. This is all just experience. You wait!' and he paused to savour the prospect. 'She'll go back to Stoverville and lay it waste.'

Mrs Bird passed the examinations which qualified her as a realtor with inordinately high marks. Then, her certificate in her bag and her training indelibly stamped in her mind, she descended on the Stoverville real estate market like a shrike upon doves. She took a bachelor apartment on the east side of town, got herself accepted as a saleswoman by the newest and most alert broker in town, and began to prowl all over town in her car, late into the evenings, making notes on the houses and affairs of all the people she knew, and on the prospects of their households breaking up. She knew the town and its inhabitants so well that she was better qualified than any of the other salesmen in the office.

None of the other people were Stoverville natives; they had all been shipped in from the home office in Toronto. None had so close a grasp of the local context, not even the branch manager, who came to cherish her mightily. She knew which middle-aged couple was only waiting eagerly to marry off the last plain daughter before fleeing to Florida, what pair of rich youngsters had gone through three houses already and were seeking a fourth that might conform more closely to their notion of a love nest. She could gauge precisely the size of the fading old-family fortunes which held the valuable riverfront properties along King Street East, and understood before they did themselves which dowagers would soon be obliged to seal their huge houses in order to shut off the tax drain.

She anticipated all marriages, divorces, births and deaths, and knew more vital statistics than the county registrar. Soon she was making more sales than anyone in the office, even the manager; she was the first lady realtor that Stoverville had ever seen, a kind of albatross or Moby Dick, a 'lusus naturae,' a mysterious natural phenomenon.

Aunt Cleila deplored the turn of affairs because, although she herself was very comfortably fixed, holding much acreage out in the back concessions as well as her King Street house, her income was fixed and rather small. She guessed that 'poor Ruthie' with only her tiny bachelor apartment to maintain would soon have more loose money to dispose of than she herself. She made a series of querulous phone calls around the family circle but obtained small sympathy.

Cousin Roger was wiser. He did his level best to sell Mrs Bird a Cadillac, telling her that her new position virtually dictated the purchase.

'You can take six people out to see a house at once,' he said, 'and think of the impression you'll create.'

She stared at him thoughtfully. 'What do you think of these Volkswagen station wagons?'

Cousin Roger retired in chagrin.

Of them all, Uncle Maurice pursued the wisest course. He made no overture to Mrs Bird, figuring that when she wanted to come and see him she would without being asked. Soon she was in and out of his office frequently, conferring with him on the social backgrounds of her clients. Between them, she and Uncle Maurice knew enough about Stoverville equities to jail half the town.

In Hartford, Conn., Millicent and James were left out of things almost completely. Mrs Bird came to see them very briefly when Jassy was born and then hastened back to Stoverville pleading the excuse of a pending big deal. They asked her back repeatedly but her replies were evasive until finally they saw that it was useless and stopped asking her.

Just before she climbed into the bathtub, Millicent had been reading her mother's latest evasive note. She and James had had to hire a sitter in order to enjoy one of their rare evenings out. She thought irritatedly of other people's mothers and the quantity of free baby-sitting they afforded. In her letter, Mrs Bird mentioned that she would be spending the next two weeks in Montreal, first at a realtors' convention, then in investigating the finances of a suspicious sub-divider.

She was paying for the trip with the proceeds of her next-to-last big sale. She had succeeded in moving a famous old Stoverville white elephant, a forty-room riverfront mansion that had been unoccupied for ten years and was impoverishing the owners with upkeep and tax charges. She had sold it to an order to teaching sisters as the nucleus of a convent boarding school. Her commission had been thirteen hundred. She was taking the manager of her office to dinner that night in Montreal; they had important matters to discuss.

Millicent began to shed tears, not of sorrow but of sheer

annoyance. 'I'm hopeless, I know,' she wailed in extreme irritation, 'but I can't understand mother at all.'

James thought to himself that he had no complaints; they would certainly be Mrs Bird's heirs which, though a small, mean, and distant consolation for the denial of Mrs Bird's company, was nevertheless a consolation. Unless, that is, he pondered, unless ... he was not certain of her age but thought it sufficient.

'We'll be seeing her,' he said, content to wait, 'sooner or later. She's not interested in us. Why should she be? She has other fish to fry,' and he thought of the two realtors conferring over dinner at Café Martin.

'Well, I think it's unnatural,' complained Millicent.

'It's the most natural thing in the world,' said James. He repeated it with satisfaction. 'The most natural thing in the world.'

He began to laugh to himself in a way which, he knew, always antagonized his wife.

The Changeling

ARE 'FIGARO' and 'picaro' really the same word, the clown, rogue, slyboots, *schnorrer,* and buffo hero all rolled up together in their derivation? Rory O'Leary came down from Sudbury and Copper Cliff 'with a romantic tale on his eyelashes,' with a retinue of hardrock friends who had worked underground, with a self-created legend of his prowess as a persuader of females, to flash across the vision of his college classmates as already something of a legend, though none excepting himself bore undisputed testimony to his tale. At various times he used to drop his hand of bridge and slip mysteriously out of the coffee shop, or lounge at a frozen streetcar stop in the dead of winter, to give a message or accept one from a lowering disciple who, he would tell you proudly if you chanced to bump into them, was 'just out.' Without enlarging on the phrase he made you understand that he meant 'just out of the penitentiary' – an implication which burnished his reputation as the confidant and patron of rough men.

Rory was then nineteen, a year or two older than most of the youngsters in his class, and he had a certain specious authority of statement, a trick of flatly putting an assertion so that, although you doubted it very much on the grounds of its inherent improbability, you found yourself half a believer. You swallowed his whoppers where other men's fibs would not go down.

Some of the girls, particularly Toronto girls who came and went by the day, found him attractive, even endearing, his eyelashes just long enough to bear the strain of his patent fictitiousness. They felt obscurely that he had invented himself and done a handsome job of it; he had straight thick dark blond hair which he used to flatten with water so that frizzy ends projected at the base of his skull, making him resemble a little the early Jimmy Cagney, in those days reincarnate on the late late show. Rory had small delicate ears which pressed themselves flat against the sides of his head and he had little hands and feet which were not at all delicate but seemed somehow pugnacious, and he had bloodshot whites to his eyes, heightening the impression of a picaresque wandering boyhood, and finally a mouth which, if this were not the nineteen-sixties, would best be described as 'loose.' He used to clean and clean himself; he was always taking a bath when you called for him in the college residence. It came to be something of a puzzle – why does Rory O'Leary bathe so much?

Bathe as he might his skin stayed muddy, his adolescent skin eruptions refused to quit him, and after a while he gave up hoping that he might grow taller before his majority, understanding that he would be five feet seven no matter how he exercised. His vivacity and energy buoyed him up as he linked arms confidentially with you and your girl coming down Queen's Park Crescent, letting you know that he had doubled his allowance, or lost it all, in a card game at the end of town the night before. His blue eyes would flash at your current girl, revolving the notion that you might soon be through with her and that he might 'move in' as he would express it afterwards when she had gone to her lecture. He was never the first to take a girl around, preferring to let others do the spadework; his strategy was to present himself as a superior second choice and he had some success with second-year girls on the rebound from freshman entanglements.

His paternity was of course disputed; in his first year he let it be known that he objected to the phrase 'you old bastard' not because of its profaneness but because he *was* one. He would tell you this towards the end of a beer party, sometimes objecting loudly that the term hurt him very much, sometimes threatening to go outside with you. Everyone in his year canvassed the students known to be from Sudbury and Copper Cliff (nearly the same town) but those who came from Sudbury thought that Rory must come from Copper Cliff while those from Copper Cliff maintained the reverse. It wasn't a matter of disowning or disliking him; it was mainly that nobody could pin down exactly where he did come from, although one of the two towns could certainly be assigned the distinction. He was exactly circumstantial about their streets and cafés and had been seen there by the natives.

Little by little as he knew you better, he would unfold his

story, and it turned out to be the classic tale of the frog prince awaiting his metamorphosis. He claimed that his father was a wealthy Toronto mining man; sometimes he could be quite bitter about it.

'He races a six-metre,' he would say, 'between here and Rochester, New York, but he refuses to provide for me.

You were to gather from this that his father was wealthy but not old – still vigorous and youthful like Rory himself, perhaps a Humphrey Bogart type.

'One day I'll go to him,' Rory would say, 'and he'll recognize me and acknowledge me.' One of the missing elements in this story was any very detailed treatment of Rory's mother. Nobody in either of his putative home towns had seen her, it appeared, and he would say nothing about her except that she was living, that he was thought to resemble her closely (the point of the great recognition-scene with his father) and that the undergraduate women resembled her not at all. He used to call girls for dates at nine-thirty on Friday or Saturday night, implying a disrespect that affronted them, telling them as plainly as possible that they didn't measure up to his ideal of womanhood.

'We'll call up a couple of nurses,' he might say, after drinking all Saturday afternoon, 'fill them up with liquor and see what happens.' He had a naïve faith in his physical attractions and a very deeply rooted belief in the necessary looseness of nurses in training. The General Hospital and Saint Michael's were his favourite targets late in the evening when he was without a girl. And yet he rarely succeeded in getting nurses to go out with him, a circumstance which he seemed not to notice.

Anyway he would go to his father in an oak-panelled Bay Street office. There would be a fireplace and a lot of expensive office furniture, featuring those green leather chairs with square brass nailheads. And his father would rise from behind his massive desk, his eyes filling with tears, put his hands out and, conscious of his twenty years' delinquency, mutter brokenly: 'My boy, my boy.'

Then there would be an easy job for Rory and a white Jaguar, and high fashion models whom he believed to be even more turpitudinous, if that were possible, than trained nurses.

He would be changed from Rory O'Leary the frog into Rory the prince. Meanwhile he remained a compulsive talker, never quite on the inside of any group.

NOW THE TROUBLE with a fellow like Rory is that there is no way, short of hiring detectives, to check his story, no matter how far-fetched. He might very well have a rich father who would in time pluck him out of the crush and raise him to his proper rank in society. Or he might not.

But you can't very well go up to somebody with a tale like this and ask him: 'Say, did you ever get in touch with your dad?'

It wouldn't be fitting somehow; you have to take these things on trust, no matter how incredible they are. Most people at least half trusted Rory and nobody ever came out point-blank and asked him for evidence, like a birth certificate, say, or family photographs or letters. There were a dozen mining brokers downtown who might very well have fathered a son or two in the north country before they made their strikes and became respectable. More than a dozen. Hundreds! But they had nothing to do with the university. How could their slips and lapses be collated by a group of curious and unsatisfied college boys?

It was easy to be impatient with Rory because of this unsatisfactory aspect of all his hints and gleams. In many ways his story hung together. He never contradicted himself. He *did* go home to Sudbury (or perhaps Copper Cliff) at Christmas, Easter, and in May. He did have friends from there, odd friends, who kept turning up at his side to confound his doubters. And these odd friends demonstrated a curious deference to him, sometimes, and a touching loyalty.

Take Onesime Paquette! Everybody from the university who knew Rory came in time to know Onesime as well. He was the real article – the real diamond in the rough – of Rory's tales. He had unquestionably worked underground as a hardrock miner. He knew nickel processing from the inside out – you could tell from the way he described it, when he talked at all, which was seldom. A man who works underground for INCO must have certain definite characteristics, strength and endurance first of all, and a dumb capacity to make use of them indefinitely, and a kind of simple ability to enjoy the delights of the senses without pausing to consider how long they may last. Onesime was perfect.

He wasn't a big man. He was about five feet ten, with sloping shoulders and long arms. He was not stupid by a very long way but he was calm and quiet, and quite slow. He didn't make mistakes in his reasoning and you never felt that you were talking to a child – God, no – when you talked to him. But he took a long time to think out his answers. He was unbelievably strong. It's hard to tell how strong Onesime was without appearing to exaggerate. Some illustrations: he could pick up one end of a Corvair with negligent ease with one hand without breathing hard, while somebody changed a tire. He could probably have done the same with a Cadillac. He could hold two full-grown girls above his head, one in each hand, spinning them around like Indian clubs, as a joke, and with no visible effort of any kind. One of the girls, Adrienne Summerby, not exactly a gazelle, must have weighed a solid one-fifty.

Those were little matters, practically party tricks, but he also did some other things that put all the college boys in dread of him. He came to a football game where everybody was drinking a fifty-fifty mixture of grain alcohol and eighty-cent Catawba wine, called 'tractor gas' because that's what it looked like, and at half-time he knocked two enormous policeman cold, one after the other in a matter of seconds, without removing his heavy overcoat. Neither punch travelled more than three inches.

He never said what he was doing in Toronto; he certainly had no intention of attending school or going to work. He just came down to be with Rory. They took a small apartment together near the university – Rory had moved out of residence at the beginning of third year – and were inseparable. Onesime wasn't quite Rory's bodyguard, a suggestion which would have insulted them both, but he sort of evened things up for Rory, as possession of firearm might. When there were fights in alleys, caused by Rory, he did the fighting himself but Onesime was always leaning against the wall to see that he didn't overmatch himself and get badly beaten.

All of Rory's nominal friends at school tried to get Onesime off by himself so they could be friends with him too, so that they too could say that they were friendly with northern tough guys, and also so that they could cross-examine him about Rory. He was always agreeable and would come and have a few beers with you, and even lend money sometimes. He always had money. Which was bewildering; he couldn't have saved it at INCO although they pay very well. He was exceedingly open-handed, almost ingenuous, and a few of the less provident drinkers in Rory's set were tempted to take advantage of this until they discovered that Onesime always set a precise time at which any money he loaned was to be repaid. If he said Friday p.m. at three in the King Cole Room, that's what he meant and God help you if you didn't have the money there on time.

Dave Callendar once borrowed four dollars from Onesime on a Wednesday night, knowing perfectly well that he wouldn't be able to repay the debt until the following Monday. But Dave was a light-hearted improvident fellow who always hoped that something would turn up, and so tended to ignore Onesime's deadline which in this case was Friday at three.

On Friday morning somebody charitably told Dave about Onesime's opinions on the question of deadlines and about the inevitable consequences of missing one. He had been at that football game and went ashy pale when he heard.

'But I was drunk when I promised,' he wailed.

'Doesn't make any difference to him,' somebody said helpfully.

'But I don't have any money. I was going to ask him for some more for the weekend.'

'Oh, I wouldn't do that, Dave.' Just then Rory came into the coffee shop, a thing he rarely did in his third, and last, year. Dave begged him to intercede with Onesime.

'Wouldn't do any good. You'd better get it up.'

'Can't I get an extension?'

'No.'

The upshot was that poor Dave, his bowels turned to water with fear and horror, and his head whirling with a hangover, had to travel all over town on foot, borrowing a little change from everyone he met, to raise the four dollars. He tottered into the King Cole Room at three precisely, looking as if he were about to have a coronary, and sat down limply at Onesime's table.

'Here's your money,' he said stertorously.

Onesime looked up mildly from his drink and pocketed the proffered handful of small silver.

'I was afraid you wouldn't make it,' he said mildly.

'Oh no! No, no, no. Here I am, right on time.'

'I see that,' said Onesime kindly, 'do you have any money left?'

Dave began to recover his breath and his spirits. 'No,' he said, 'but at least I've got time.'

'I'll buy you one glass of beer,' said Onesime. He did so and later on some other chaps came in and Dave was able to bum enough money for his dinner and a few more drinks. He hadn't visibly profited from the narrow escape.

THE LONGER Onesime stayed in town, and the more he and Rory grew absorbed in their mysterious connections, the less attention Rory paid to university affairs, flunking out at the end of the third year. He had had enough of sages, and cloistered halls, and books, as he said, and now he yearned for a larger sphere of activity, scope for his indistinct wish for greatness to express itself. He was seen less and less in the coffee shop and when he came there he displayed a certain contempt – no, not contempt, disdain, for he was incapable of contempt – for the childish concerns of college boys. He was in a hurry to put aside childish things and go about his father's business.

But there was, as it happens, a spectacularly childish windup to his college career. He and Onesime were on a party in the course of which it was agreed amongst the revellers that they should go and beat up their host's former landlord, a man of low inclinations and motives who had thrown this host out of his boarding house on account of noisy parties.

There was a lengthy contentious debate about how the churl should be lured out onto his front porch where the beating would be administered. Rory and Onesime began to wrestle and to disagree, at first jokingly and then half seriously. They rolled downstairs and out onto the lawn where they began to spar slowly, surrounded by Rory's college friends who had been waiting for this.

'All right,' exclaimed Rory excitedly, 'all right, you want to fight, come on, we'll go where we can fight.' They called a cab and drove off, perfectly amicably, to High Park, unaccompanied. There they dismissed the cab driver and began to box in earnest. Onesime shattered Rory's jaw with his first serious punch, then they shook hands tearfully and went home on perfectly good terms. But Rory's jaw had to be wired and he was unable for some weeks to speak effectively. Some thought this a good thing but most were amused and sorry for him. Onesime indicated neither remorse nor triumph nor in fact much interest in the injury. Amongst the real hardrocks, he implied by his silence, such things were regular, scarcely worthy of notice. Anyway the injury marked the end of Rory's higher education.

He meant to go into finance and company promotion, he told everyone when he regained his powers of speech, though what imaginable capacities he might have for this line of work were never clear to his audience. He had no information, no capital, no training; he couldn't add or subtract numbers in more than three places. What he did have, and what might have made him a great and renowned success, was a boundless indefinite optimism, an ability to stare reality in the face, and miss it, such as few of us possess any more. He would outline his plans in the broadest of terms, the broad view was apparently the *sine qua non*.

'What are you going to do? How will you get along?' Adrienne Summerby asked him in great annoyance. She was trying to break things off with him and wanted an excuse.

'Get along?'

'Yes, yes,' she said, impatient and flustered, 'get along, eat, live.'

He looked at her with round blue eyes and lifted the back of his hand to his mouth. 'Well, I always have,' he said, 'so far.' The question had never come up before.

'How?'

He hadn't bought any new clothes for years; he had a blue-grey tweed jacket for good clothes and ratty sweaters for every day. 'I get an allowance,' he said.

She burned to demand where it came from, who supplied it and why, but naturally couldn't. The closest she came was to ask irritatedly, 'Isn't it ever going to stop?'

'When I'm twenty-five,' he said serenely, 'it'll stop when I'm twenty-five.'

She didn't ask him how he knew the date with such precision, or in what legally witnessed agreement the end of his father's responsibility was set down. Like everyone else she didn't know what to think about his father.

'What then?' she asked, telling herself that she did not mean to be a mother to Rory O'Leary; he had parents enough already.

'I'll be in business by myself.' He obviously had some model of lightning success in mind, some boy wolf of Bay Street. 'I believe I'll go into base metals,' he said, as if to enlighten her.

'Good luck,' she said briefly, trying to grasp what it was about him that moved her feelings; it wasn't as though she cared about him at all.

'Or maybe vanadium,' he said, lost in contemplation of his brilliant future, 'vanadium alloys can be put to limitless uses. Last year production was up a hundred and thirty-five percent.'

'Stop making these things up!' she said, close to tears and furious with herself.

'I'm not making them up.' He pulled a Department of Mines leaflet from his pocket. 'It says so right here.' Every now and then (and it was one of his most characteristic actions) he would confound you by knowing exactly what he was talking about, and the accuracy of the particular bit of information always shaded off at the edges into some perversely unreal scheme. He knew the name 'vanadium.' Did he know what the stuff was, where it might be found, what you would use it for when you got it out of the ground? There was no way to find out.

It was on this refusal of his hearers to ask the blasting questions that he must always have relied.

HE DISAPPEARED downtown for a while, maybe to have the

crucial interview with his father, maybe not. There was never anything sensational in the papers, not even a legal announcement disavowing responsibility for his debts. His father, obstinately concealed from sight, never manifested himself, never set Rory up in business, never did anything for him that anybody heard about, there was no good news. If there were to be high fashion models and white Jaguars, they would have to be created by Rory himself; nobody ever helped him to them.

Did the grotesque vulgarity of the imaginary recognition-scene prevent its actuality, or was his father only a desperate stock-jobber whom Rory didn't dare approach for fear of having his dubieties confirmed? Or was he rich and embarrassed and implacable? And the mother, was she a brown Indian maiden from around Sudbury – there are such people – or an all-night sandwich girl in the Dial Lunch or the heiress of an old prospecting family, or what was she anyway, married or single, a seductress or a poor virgin victimized?

Life is composed of epiphanies and departures. Heroes and heroines are always coming and going, appearing suddenly in a blaze of glory that forbids the sight and as suddenly removing themselves from the worshipful stare of the beholders. We find the type of the thing, naturally, in the New Testament, 'and again a little while and ye shall see me.' The wonderful aspect of the demi-god is the depth of his truth behind the dazzling appearance. Who knows, who knows, there might have been something substantial to poor Rory after all, he certainly came and went mysteriously enough and at his first disappearance was almost forgotten by his associates, there being no cult and no prediction of his eventual return. But he did come back uptown after a while, wearing a brown businessman's suit and beginning to sport the smallest of jowls.

He had gone, he told everyone, into the office of the promoter Stafford Little (at whose name the SEC still trembles) as an idea-man; he had a desk on the twentieth floor of the Royal Bank Building, up under the cornice in a tiny suite of rooms from whence he surveyed all the kingdoms of the world, the base metals situation, and mining securities generally. His principal was part investment counsellor, part hired rumour-monger, part stock salesman, mostly crook, although Rory didn't explicitly lay down the last of these elements. What they did together was vague to his hearers but then what one's friends do for a living is always unclear. Drop in on your oldest buddy in his office and observe him at work. You wouldn't recognize him, would you, as 'Mr Smith' to the surly receptionist who asks your name and business and reluctantly lets you pass. Your friend wears a jacket and tie, and talks persistently into the phone in your presence about matters of which you know nothing, they aren't part of the life you and he have shared. And as you come away from his office feeling rebuffed you remember that he has never seen you efficiently doing what you do, and you think that he would be pretty impressed too. So it goes. Nobody had any idea what an idea-man for a petty promoter was meant to do but the new suit and the new flesh under the chin were oddly impressive.

'I'm not a partner yet,' he would say, ebulliently, 'but I expect to be any time.'

'Don't you have to invest some money?'

'Not in this business,' he would say happily, and his hearers would tremble. 'All you need is your creativity. You've got to be ahead of everybody else.' And then he would bend his head down tight over his leather-bound portfolio and look up at you almost craftily from under his lashes. 'I have here,' he might propose, 'reports on some vanadium veins in Ecuador that you wouldn't believe, and nobody knows about them.' To do him credit, he never tried to sell you anything, leaving that to his boss, who controlled the sucker lists and the Addressograph plates.

ONE BRIGHT morning last March he took a taxi uptown from the Royal Bank Building in a state of extreme elation, and burst in on Onesime, who still shared his apartment and who customarily slept till noon. Rory had been promising to work his friend in on the first thing that looked both good and safe, and this, as it seemed, was it.

'Get up,' he shouted excitedly, 'get up and get your clothes on. Pack an overnight bag. I've got your ticket here.' He did, too, an airline ticket in the unmistakable blue paper folder.

In his slow confiding way, Onesime had been relying on

Rory to fit him into the operation somewhere (without prejudice) that wouldn't leave him open to later prosecution, and when he saw the airlines ticket and the taxicab waiting below his window, he asked no questions but shaved and dressed hurriedly, seized a club bag, threw an extra shirt and his shaving kit into it and rode with Rory to the airport.

Rory said a lot of excited things about their being first on the ground and about the necessity of dispatch. But all that Onesime could remember when he thought it over afterwards was the parting shouted phrase, which he could scarcely decipher over the engines.

'Wait for instructions in Mexico City,' bellowed Rory from the ground, his hands cupped to his mouth. Then the plane began to taxi out to the runway and Onesime settled back to enjoy the free ride. When they were in the air, breakfast was served, a good breakfast with eggs and bacon, not the toasted Danish and coffee they sometimes give you, and he was in very good spirits, though a bit confused. He was still half asleep.

There was a two-hour wait in New York for the plane to Mexico City and it was at Idlewild that Onesime first realized that he had only the money that was in his trousers pockets from last night. He thought of buying his lunch in the terminal but decided to defer the meal until he was in the air, on the chance that the airline would come through handsomely. Alas, he was on an afternoon run, during which no true mealtime occurred, so he went without food, except for crackers and tea, all the way to Mexico City.

He naturally expected to find money, instructions, some details about where he was headed, his passport and visas, and the other necessities for an expedition into the interior, at the desk in the terminal at Mexico City, but there was nothing. Nothing at 7:00 p.m. when he arrived, nothing at midnight when he was feeling very hungry. Nothing the next morning when he was famished. He didn't dare spend the three or four dollars he had in his pocket until he received his supplies and he had to beg for permission to pass the night on a bench in the waiting room. There was an electric outlet in the washroom, so he could shave, and there were free soap and towels. But so far there was neither money nor food, and worse still no legal identification, no return ticket, no notion of what he was supposed to be doing.

The fact was that Rory had put up the money for a one-way ticket out of his own pocket, meaning to get him on his way as fast as possible, to surprise the competition and place an experienced miner on the site where the vanadium deposits were supposed to be located, up-country in Ecuador. Onesime was to survey the lie of the land, the mining site, the distance to the railhead, and compare them with what he was used to in Copper Cliff (the establishment of one of the great giants of mining). If the operation seemed at all feasible, Rory and his boss would make a try for control of the stock issue, as usual without cash changing hands.

But Stafford Little wasn't as enthusiastic about Onesime's jaunt as Rory was. In vain did Rory plead the urgency of sending aid and comfort to their man in Mexico City. In vain did he urge the necessity of daring and vigour in their activities. The promoter grunted sourly and refused to spend a cent on a project which, he insisted, Rory had invented to embarrass him.

'But what will I do about our advance man?'

'Your advance man,' said Little resentfully, 'you got him into it, you can get him out.'

'But are you certain you don't want him to go ahead?'

'What the hell,' said the boss, angered by Rory's pertinacity, 'what the hell! What do you want to go and get mixed up in vanadium exploration for? There's nothing in that for us.'

'If we could tie it up,' said Rory, speaking hesitantly for the first time in his life, 'we'd be in on the ground floor and the stock is bound to rise.'

'Why?'

'Why?'

'Yes, why?'

'Well, it always does after a big find.'

Stafford Little gazed stonily at innocent Rory for perhaps thirty seconds. 'God,' he ejaculated at length. He paced around and around the grubby inner office where he hid from the clients.

'Do you know who you'd be dealing with, if you controlled a major vanadium deposit?' he inquired sombrely.

'No,' said Rory perkily, 'the small investor?'

'The Steel Company of Canada, that's who, and United States Steel. Do you think you're going to put something over on them?'

'But if the stuff is there ...'

'If it's there, they'll pay what it's worth, not a cent more. There's nothing in a practical mining development for us. So forget about it and, by the way, you'd better yank your buddy out of Mexico City before he gets homesick.'

'You ought to help pay his way.'

'Perhaps, but I don't intend to.'

While these debates were going forward – they took about ten days altogether, for Rory's fancies died slowly – Onesime was living in the airport waiting-room, sleeping on the benches and trying to keep himself presentable, and bumming food from the coffee counter. He had exhausted his original four dollars in three days although he had stretched and stretched it. Nearly a week later he was beginning to think he'd been forgotten. As he didn't know what the original plan had been he was unable to conjecture what had gone awry. All he could do was sit and wait, picking up illustrated magazines that were left lying around, they were mainly in Spanish, and hoping that somebody would remember him and send for him.

Early on the ninth day of his exile, the sun hit him in the eyes as he lay on his bench, shocking him into wakefulness. He rolled stiffly around on his side and into a sitting position, feeling older than his years. Then he rubbed his hands into his eyes, feeling dizzy, and when they cleared and he could see he noticed an elderly woman sitting near him, staring at him peculiarly.

'Do you live here, young man?' she said in English.

'No, lady, I'm just stopping over.'

'You were here when I came to arrange about my ticket, that's three days ago. Haven't you anywhere else to sleep? Why don't you go to a hotel?'

This woman reminded him of his mother so he was open with her, describing his uneasy situation rather fully.

'My gracious,' she exclaimed as he told her, 'such a nice

young man as you are. This man O'Leary sounds like a villain to me.'

Onesime hastened to correct her impression.

'From Toronto, too,' she said wonderingly, 'isn't that a coincidence, that's where I come from. I'm down here on my holiday to see the cathedral, the oldest in the New World, it's truly lovely, isn't it? But of course you haven't seen it.'

'No,' he said, guiltily, 'no, I didn't get over there.'

'I'm going home this morning,' she said, 'and I'll tell you what I'm going to do. I can't buy you a ticket because I haven't much money left but I can give you a little bit, enough to buy a few meals, and I'll certainly see that your friend, as you call him, looks after you.' She shook hands with him, palpitatingly, and in a few minutes her plane was announced and she was carried off. Onesime went, after he washed up, to the lunch counter where he enjoyed the largest single meal he'd had since he left Toronto. It was Sunday, and he felt bad about missing Mass twice in a row; he wished that he'd at least seen the cathedral, there were postcards of it on sale in the waiting room and he thought it looked beautiful.

The next morning, Monday morning and therefore not a good morning, Rory was sitting at his desk on the twentieth floor attempting to compose his thoughts to face and outwit the problems of a puzzling week ahead, when all at once this strange unknown elderly woman appeared, absolutely out of nothingness, and began to belabour him about the shoulders and head with a rolled umbrella.

'You're a false friend and a wicked man,' she declared loudly, and he winced, 'to play such a trick on Mr Paquette. A traitor, do you hear? Now you march right over to the ticket office and send him his fare home. No, no I won't listen to your smooth excuses, you're going to do it before I leave you alone.'

Rory had many things on his mind besides Onesime's bad luck, including subpoenas, court appearances, jail, so he crouched there bewildered, sweating, while she cudgelled him with her umbrella, trying to tell her that he hadn't the money for a ticket and didn't know what to do.

'You'd find the sum soon enough, if it were one of your

young women,' she said, 'or a horserace. Now I want to see you settle this at once; there are ways to raise money and I won't leave until you do something.'

He couldn't have the police throw her out because they'd unquestionably take her side, and she simply wouldn't go away. In the end she came with him on a visit to the finance company where he extended an already existing obligation unhealthily far. Then she herded him along to the airlines office and at last into a phone booth where he spent a vast sum in silver placing an encouraging call to Mexico City. They got through finally and it was almost worth the money to hear the relief in Onesime's voice; it eased Rory's conscience and, after the nice old lady whose name he never caught had gone, he felt good about what he'd done. Despite his other cares, which pressed upon him very heavily, Onesime had been getting on his mind the last week.

When he met his friend that night, in their dirty little apartment, it was almost – almost – as if the incident hadn't happened. Onesime had lost three or four pounds and had a severe cold in the back but that was all.

'Those benches were very hard,' he murmured in mild reproach, and then he went to bed and slept for fourteen hours.

RORY SAT loosely, like a rag doll, on the couch in the living room, telling himself hopefully at first that he had gotten off lightly from this escapade at least. He hadn't exactly been afraid that Onesime would take another swing at his vulnerable jaw. They both knew that it was weak where it had been wired and couldn't stand another blow. But he had been afraid that Onesime might give up on him, and realize that Rory was never going to help him to anything.

There was a limit to Onesime's loyalty, he began to guess at last, and maybe this time he had reached it. He looked soberly around the room, feeling peculiarly disconnected, as though he were watching a speeded-up movie.

He wondered idly what had happened to his plan, sitting cross-legged on the ragged divan that half filled the room. He had been about to make a lot of easy money, in two or three ways that he had proudly invented and counted on, and all at once the prizes had been snatched from his reach; they always were, all the prizes like the most expensive ornaments on a Christmas tree, glittering up at the starry top.

He examined the depressing room and reluctantly saw it as it was, the holes in the worn carpet, the smelly ashtrays, the dirty Woolworth dishes piled in unpredictable corners. Always before this he had been able to ignore his surroundings, certain that they were illusory and would vanish presently, to be superseded by something very grand. As he stared at the cigarette burns in the divan they suddenly projected themselves forward, coming to meet him, seeming real and inescapable. He listened to Onesime's peaceful snores and felt afraid.

But he had trained himself, with religious fervour, never to compromise, never to settle for what was obviously attainable. What he could easily have, the small apartment, the ashes and the dishes, was not acceptable. What associates would the denizen of such a place enjoy, what girls, what hopes, what dinner-coated entrepreneurs? He had planned to continue assuming the transitory character of his present residence, still and forever faithful that his transformation was close at hand.

He thought of taking a hot relaxing bath, scrubbing himself with his special castile soap that didn't bother his skin. Getting to his feet he went and looked at Onesime. What happened inside that hard head when someone betrayed him? It would take his old friend at least a week to see how he had been treated, and then he would go back to Sudbury and when he did Rory's reputation would sink very low. It was not right – he saw it at last – to throw your friend off to sink or swim. He could tell himself with nearly perfect justice that he had always acted kindly towards Onesime, and telling himself, he saw the illegitimate condescension as clearly as he'd seen the cigarette burns.

Who was he to condescend to Onesime, or Adrienne or Stafford Little, or to anybody? Why did everybody always act as though he were somebody? Because he had himself, because he was his father's son, because he had intimated his great expectations. All fiction. Not lies, he told himself defiantly, not lies. I have a father who has helped me through school, who gave me an allowance till I was twenty-five, who still has money and will give me some, a little anyway, but that's all. It reduces itself to a commonplace legal claim. And he has other sons, legitimate, with a precedent claim on him. He stood leaning against the bedroom door and looked at Onesime with affection and fear, knowing his man too well. Onesime would go home.

In a couple of weeks, Rory bought him a ticket, a railway ticket this time, sending him off in style, trying to make it up to him. They would continue friends, they told each other, but the glamour was gone. Onesime didn't believe any more that Rory was going to wave his wand over him and make him a plant manager. They stood in Union Station waiting for the night train and spoke very little.

'I wish you would let me know what job you get. I hope the employment situation is good. You'll be making more money than I am, kiddo, twice as much.'

'I'll be gang boss,' said Onesime, looking at his ticket.

'That at least. Would you like me to wire the employment office?'

'No, don't do that,' said Onesime, and Rory felt deflated. He had no influence of any kind at INCO and acted as though he did out of mere habit.

'Drop me a card,' he said, as they came to the gate.

'I'll send the money for the ticket,' Onesime said glumly.

'You don't have to.'

'You can't afford it, Rory.' They shook hands and Onesime disappeared upstairs.

Rory took the subway uptown as fast as he could. He went at once to the King Cole Room partly for old times' sake, mainly in the expectation of finding somebody he knew to talk to. He came in from the street with his hair flying, his cheeks flushed, his overcoat unbuttoned, looking the picture of youthful verve, almost unchanged from what he had been at nineteen, unless you happened to know that he was nearing thirty. In possession of that special information, you were able to see how he was thickening through the waist. You took note of the inch of pink scalp visible where his hairline had been.

Since you knew him, you sat back and waited for the story,

and of course he couldn't keep it back, for the fun of the thing. He was being sued – fortunately it was a civil action, although a prosecution for fraud was threatened and might follow. He told you at length, flashing his eyes and twisting his lips oddly, about the hilarious muddle he had perpetrated in the courtroom. They couldn't understand, in court, that he had no earthly claim to the disputed securities. And therefore they couldn't believe that he had passed them off as his own, and even offered to sell them. He had been severely censured by the presiding judge for his conduct; but the censure had carried less force that it might because Judge MacEwan couldn't help chuckling incredulously at the boldness and total knavery of his behaviour. Luckily it had been a relatively small matter.

This grotesque yarn, which he used for months to avoid being quizzed about Onesime, seemed to his auditors a penultimate flicker before his light went out and he settled down like the rest of us to earning his slow way, comfort always two jumps ahead. That yarn was true. He had been wide open to prosecution but his acts had been so naïvely dreadful that he was allowed to go free, apparently on the theory that he wouldn't dare try it again, and he didn't. The Boy Wolf of Bay Street never hunted again.

Rory grows thicker and balder these days, and seems shorter in proportion to his weight. He's very easy to talk to; you can gossip scandalously about your friends, saying things you wouldn't dare say to their faces. And when he passes these remarks along, nobody minds. Nobody cares what he says in front of Rory O'Leary; it's understood that nobody means a word of it. Because he's nobody. He's a frog who's successfully resisted all the magic and will remain a frog to the end.

A Season of Calm Weather

IF A GREAT INSTITUTION be not reverend, worthy, and venerable, its most prudent course (allowing it to possess a corporate genius, character, or intelligence) will be to assume to itself the outward and visible seemings of these qualities, that they may be publicly received as of its essence.

The University of Burlington is neither a fit object of reverence, nor a consciously moral agency, nor yet very ancient, having been founded in the year 1842 as the first city college on this continent, and as what was then an oddity, an institution of higher learning without ecclesiastical ties. Disembarrassed of these trailings, the University began at once to display, as if the workings of a hovering daimon, an enormous aptitude for associating to itself professors and institutes of every mode of science except the theological, so that it has always been in the van of the march of mind so characteristic of the later nineteenth and twentieth centuries.

In psychophysics after Fechner, in linguistics after Boas and Sapir, the University of Burlington has domiciled and comforted the newest learning, endowed its professors, circulated its transactions and proceedings, and even, let it be admitted at once, bred up a corps of native theorists which displays coherent intellectual habits.

'The Burlington school of intellectual historians' was the label employed by one of their number, more venturesome and less reticent than the rest, to denominate the group in his three-volume history of the higher learning in America. And indeed intellectual history of a severely technical sort in whatever discipline, whether economics or philology or ethereal theory from Newton to Michelson and Morley, has been the learned procedure most often practised by 'the Burlington school.' *The Journal of the March of Mind,* referred to in bibliographies as *JMM,* was founded just after the First World War in honour of this corporate modality and ranks highest among the eclectic quarterlies – those devoted to a point of view rather than to a special study. In the pages of *JMM* one discovers inquiries of every scientific and humane sort, their only similarity a certain dry and nearly clerical deportment which is peculiar and striking. For the institution which grew up as professedly secular, and connected with neither priesthood nor cult, has begun to grow its own – acolytes at least – and almost celebrants. There *is* such a thing as 'a Burlington man' recognizable by his sanity, his safeness, his reserve, his method, his learned eminence, his distrust of novelty, his rigour, O tower of ivory, O house of gold.

The university has displayed its quasi-biological assimilative powers in a multitude of ways; its finances have always flourished. Its alumni are as the sands of the shore, and properly grateful. Its determinedly neutral ideological stance has lured the donations of the business community, which commonly distrusts academies of less guarded coloration. The University of Burlington is therefore enormously wealthy and its diversity of scope and structure has become bewildering.

Here is the Centre for Area Studies in Hausa and Tchad Culture and Linguistics. Here are divers research teams in the social sciences, each with its grant of half a million. Here is an atomic reactor, and here the largest mechanical brain. And here before them all, the adornment of the University of Burlington, and the only one of its associated institutions which it permits to confer advanced degrees under its aegis but without review, here is the internationally famous Institute for Ontology and Phenomenology founded in 1929 by Burlington's most distinguished – and most atypical – son, the metaphysician Francis X. Devlin, M.A. (Burlington) and *licencié ès lettres* (Louvain), the friend and student of Husserl, the librarian of his great master's papers, and first president, though not now president, of the institute which he called into being.

THE POSTULATES break down and away; one merely sees and need not discourse upon the vision afterwards unless the clamour of the aspirants around one call forth speech. One sees perpetually and there is no tense in any language adequate to express the efflorescence of being. Being. I tell my travelling companion that I will meet him in St. Pancras Station under the clock in eleven months and three days at noon, and in the fullness of time I go and he is there, the thing works. Wonderful!

Time runs forward according to our metaphors, there being no reason why it should not run backward equally well unless we allow that causes necessarily precede effects, temporally as well as logically, and that this certain number of causes once existent will produce in successive temporal collisions these effects and no others. Why not the other way round, the effect productive of the cause, the multiplicity of effects shrinking into the single cause like a film run backwards? Mr Disney exhibits the growth of the plant in the slowest motion, the leaves exfoliating, the stem growing longer and thicker before our eyes. Why should not the wide leaves and the thick stem affect the knotted bud beneath the ground? The gnarled aged multiplex of effects in the House of Providence reduce regressively to the baby in the hospital nursery, its history always narrowing? Or again why need there be successivity at all, why not indeed an indefinite arrangement of sequences in non-spatial relations? This becomes mathematics and does not engage me. True causes and effects are simultaneous and co-ordinate, the one in the other, the other in the one (Leibniz). But he was right; they are somehow annexed, and are to be seen together, not together in space but together in form. This is too weak; they are not together. They are one, the cause and the effect are identical. Billiard ball A becomes billiard ball B if, and only if, absolute contact occurs instead of mere collision. Might I observe absolute contact with an electron microscope, perhaps, or with some enormously subtle weighing machine – might I calculate how many subatomic particles were deposited inside billiard ball B?

Why do I see so clearly that absolute contact implies identity? Why is it that I know that the spheres would cohere if they touched, really touched, instead of simply approaching each other nearly? Bread becomes flesh when assimilation takes place. Absolute contact is a biological category and not a physical, though the new biology claims to be physics of a sort. Is this a mistake, and is not life the condition of absolute contact? If the billiard balls were identical in physical properties, as mass, location, force, there could only be one of them (Leibniz again) but we do not observe that billiard balls ever grow together, however one compresses them. Why?

I see and claim to understand why but I cannot tell why. No words express identity. Diderot, Freud, Hegel tell us that man is *double,* all of them dissenting from Leibniz who knew so much about identities. How double? If an identity were double, it could be described in the language of physics; but we see that it cannot and in any case an entity may be one, or three or more, but may not be simply *double.* If you will not accept unity as identity, you must accept trinity. Two will not suffice because between any two things, even the only two things in the universe, even if we think away time and space and arrive at two absolutely unconditioned beings, between two things coexistent in any sense there is necessarily a third mode of being – relation – unless we suppose two universes in one of which the other is non-existent, and vice versa, like the matter and antimatter of naïve physics – and even here relation. If there is more than one thing, there must be more than two, the least being three, avoid theology, avoid it. I may be a Trinitarian in religion but need not be Hegelian in ontology.

LATE THOUGHTS of an old man's mind, late appearance of the metaphysical appetite.

WHEN FRANCIS X. DEVLIN came back to Burlington at the age of thirty-four, in the fateful year 1929, the times and circumstances conspired artfully to effect the foundation of the Institute of Ontology and Phenomenology, the project next his heart and mind. The university had grown immensely wealthy in the preceding decade, the benefactions of its stock-jobbing alumni generous beyond every expectation, the insane behaviour of traders on margin conditioning the establishment of a philosophical academy. The officers of the university allowed him first an old house on a tract they meant soon to develop as men's residences, fancying that the new establishment would be an idle and transitory appendage to the university. In this they were mistaken. For in addition to the providential state of the stock market, the evolution of American philosophical opinion seemed to conspire towards the deep rooting and swift growth of the new academy.

Devlin, president of the institute and disciple of Husserl, had published while still at Louvain his only book, *L'intentionnalité et la connaissance de l'être trans-objectif, chez Brentano,* and one or two copies of this short but important work had found their way home and been circulated subterraneously in professional circles. In addition he was known to have contributed two seminal papers to the *Jahrbuch für Philosophie und Phänomenologische Forschung* though no one had as yet seen them. He had been the trusted friend of the master, and the correspondent of Bergson, Benda, and Maritain. When, in late 1928, Husserl had given up his chair at Fribourg to be succeeded by a disciple whose tendencies he deeply mistrusted, Martin Heidegger, it was his correspondence with Devlin at Louvain which first drew his attention to the Belgian seat of learning and which ultimately led to the deposit of his archives there at the wish of his widow.

Devlin had gone to Louvain intending to study the new scholasticism as an intellectual historian. He returned to America the first transcendental phenomenologist ever to grace these shores and was fondly regarded as such by every moulder of philosophical opinion in the hemisphere. By 1933 every variety of radical empiricism had been examined by American philosophers, and been rejected by many of the most advanced. Phenomenology, the professed mediator between radical empiricism and absolute idealism, with hints of aid and comfort even for naïve realists, began to catch on. For there are fashions as well amongst philosophers as amongst the followers of the *haute couture.*

The Institute for Ontology and Phenomenology flourished, attracted students at a very advanced level, and by 1937, a scant eight years after its foundation, was internationally known and respected, so that in that year the institute was first allowed to confer the doctoral degree of the University of Burlington, without review by the administrators of the faculty of graduate studies, a circumstance which did not endear Frank Devlin to some of his colleagues.

'He's a brilliant teacher,' admitted the Dean of the faculty of graduate studies, 'but what has he written? That one book in French, I know, a hundred and thirty pages, and two articles in German.'

'But look at his influence on the students!'

'Oh, certainly, certainly, but when a brilliant teacher is dead, what is there left? He takes his insights with him.'

'Like Socrates?'

'Yes,' said the Dean, 'look what happened to him!'

It certainly seemed that the students at the institute did not publish a great deal, and they were a curiously mixed lot. Of the first five to take the institute's doctoral degree, just before the Second World War, one became an existentialist theologian, one a depth psychiatrist, one found his way back through Brentano to Thomism and disappeared, one died a hero in the war, and the last, Henry Boscawen, eventually succeeded Frank Devlin in the presidency of the institute, superseding the metaphysician of untransmissible, and hence useless, intuition by a thoroughgoing 'Burlington man.' Alone amongst the first five doctors, Boscawen published extensively; but he published no transcendental reductions of experience. He published intellectual histories for he was a disciple, not of Devlin, but of the great French historian of philosophy Amédée Souverain, Professor of the Collège de France and the distinguished author of two dozen volumes, amongst them *Le Kantianisme, La genèse et les effets de l'idéalisme du dix-neuvième siècle, Le Christ dans la pensée de G.W.F. Hegel,* and ever so many others.

Souverain had come to America in 1937 to deliver the annual Walter Gibbs Marshall Lectures in natural theology and, attracted to Burlington by the nascent, more than nascent, renown of the new little institute, he consented to deliver a half-year course in theories of the structure of the ego, a subject well within his self-imposed methodological limitations. He came at the behest of Frank Devlin himself, and his first course was an enormous success. Here, it was felt in some quarters and even by one or two of Devlin's students, was rigorous method of the Burlington stamp. Here was unimpeachable documentation, here were unquestioned facts, birth and death dates, quotation in a late text of an early text, successive editions which might be collated for evidence of change in the writer's opinions. Here was science, and what was phenomenological reduction?

Poetry, thought some, mere poetry because without data!

Just at this inopportune time, in the spring of 1938, Frank Devlin decided to go over to Belgium for a year to assist Mme Husserl in the arrangement of her late husband's archives. He was to be gone more than a year as things turned out, arriving home two weeks before the outbreak of the war. He had found the Husserl papers in an admirable state of arrangement, as he would have expected of his old master, and had simply made arrangements for their housing, editing, and publication. But the eighteen months that he spent in Europe caused him to be somewhat out of touch with the latest American developments in his field.

And the onset of war shook him sadly, troubled him and blighted his vision. He had been in constant correspondence with his master during the thirties and knew intimately Husserl's growing preoccupation with the philosophy of history and with 'the crisis of European humanity.' He had even assisted the master in formulating some of his most inward conclusions on the question, had suggested ways in which the laws of just social evolution might be purified in thought, when once the 'bracketing' of lived history were accomplished. But the master had died too soon in 1938 and as if only the hard thought of phenomenologists everywhere had kept it off, the destruction began almost as if a signal had been given.

If physical and moral evil constitute, as classical metaphysics supposes, a grievous wound in Being, a fundamental ontological deprivation, then by how much must the universe have seemed, to Francis Devlin and others with a similar gift, shrunken, violated, impaired, by the war? By any war? By the Bomb? By mass sin?

He grew silent and his lectures lost their illumination. In his thirties he had had the divine faculty that the metaphysician must have if he is to be at all a social being; he had been able to communicate, though very slowly and only with great hardship, some parts of his own apprehension. But as he drew on into middle age, and as the war engulfed continent after continent, something happened to his screen of vision, some loss of clarity, even perhaps a wavering of faith, a shuddering of his love for the radiance of the trans-objective subject (always the focus of his ontology) and an arrest in the restoration of his spirit.

The institute held classes of course, and conferences, and the composition of small doctoral theses proceeded slowly, and more slowly as more and more embryonic philosophers enlisted. It is a fact that the institute's sons compiled a distinguished war record, two of them rising to the grade of general officer. But this distinction didn't seem to assuage the wounded spirits of the school's chief.

This lapse into silence, this enfeeblement of his powers of vision, had more direct consequences in the great public world of affairs than is usually the case with philosophers' hesitations. When the journal of the movement, *Philosophy and Phenomenological Research* direct descendant of the old *Jahrbuch,* was founded at Buffalo in 1940, neither Devlin himself nor any of his students contributed anything of importance in print. They served on committees and did editorial work, to be sure, and even some of the shorter book reviews. But the heart and soul of the movement was not actively present in the composition of its journal, and this circumstance took off some of the glitter from the development. Then too when the celebrated Harvard Symposium appeared in honour of Husserl in the same year 1940, under the editorship of Farber, the names of Devlin and his principal associates were again absent.

They might, and privately did, protest that they were being perfectly true to the memory of their master by remaining silent through the year that France fell, the year of the Blitzkrieg and the apparent European triumph of barbarism. They might ask themselves how they could possibly publish insignificant formalized studies out of the depths of their horror, how philosophers could remain technical and continue to 'produce' through 'the crisis of European humanity' – that crisis which is still unresolved, which has been frozen like the frozen heart of the metaphysician for two decades. And so they contributed nothing to the movement and spoke little at the philosophic congresses, all of them dominated by the crudest instrumentalism anyway, and six years of war slipped along and Devlin and his foundation began to lapse into obscurity, a development which irritated the officers of the University of Burlington profoundly. They began to look quietly around for a possible successor to their crippled seer, and by the merest chance had not far to look.

In defiance of the Nazi authorities, exhibiting the noblest bravery and devotion to scientific and intellectual integrity, the great historian Souverain had continued to deliver his public lectures in Paris for the first two years of the Occupation, lectures which condemned, exposed, traced to its roots, humiliated the tyranny, and the tyrant too. For Souverain knew historically all the shoddy fakery, the disreputable philosophical trappings of the totalitarian régime, and he stood out on the lecture platform for two dangerous years and proclaimed these things. Then, when he had grown acutely obnoxious to the authorities, he sank out of sight and eventually reappeared in America where he was greeted as what he really was, a hero of the integrity of the intellectual process. He knew some things.

That Devlin knew them better, so much better that he found them unspeakable and couldn't lecture, was not likely to engage the affections or the votes of those officers of the university who held in their hands the disposition of the headship of their precious famous faltering institute.

And when, after the Liberation, Souverain was named Membre de l'Académie Française and refused to accept an academic post in his native country until she should have purged herself of collaborationism, the prize – that plum of reputation – had grown too great for the conscience of the University of Burlington to put it by. They proposed, in short, to supersede Devlin, whose star had gone by, with the great and famous intellectual historian. That this was a rape of the traditions built up by the institute in its short history they did not consider or even understand, for they wanted a name, and a name they must have. Devlin had obstinately preserved silence, so Devlin must go. They gave their suffrages to Souverain and he, to do him every justice, refused to supplant Devlin in his own person. Instead he proposed that the fifth of those early doctoral candidates, now Brigadier General Henry Boscawen, an intellectual historian of his own stamp who had already published four volumes (two in the two years since his discharge from the Marines) should be elected to the presidency, that he himself should remain as visiting professor, and that Devlin too should be allowed professorial rank. His proposals were enthusiastically received and the governors of the university sent him as their emissary to inform the moping phenomenologist of their deliberations and decisions. It was a sober interview.

'My dear friend,' began poor Souverain with reluctance, 'you have confused metaphysics with mystical contemplation, have you not? And they are after all distinct, and a scholar may not maintain so long a silence.'

Devlin stared at him dully. 'I see nothing to incite speech,' he said, 'and as for the confusion you intimate – it may exist in your mind. It finds no room in mine. There is no similarity whatsoever between mystical vision and the natural intuition of Being.'

'Their practical results are the same. In either case you remain rapt and silent.'

'Ontology induces no raptures! When have I ever been rapt and ecstatic? I am not a saint and do not profess to be one. And why do you introduce this question of "practical results" and silence? The "practical result" – if we are to insist on the words – the "practical result" of metaphysics is always silence.'

'Forgive me,' said Souverain, 'but that is nonsense. Metaphysics is *for* humanity. Metaphysics is to teach, is to lead others towards its own light. And its "practical results" – and I do insist on the words – are clear. Books, metaphysical books and other writings, which one can examine and from which one can learn. A philosopher is obliged in conscience to communicate the results of his researches, just as all the other members of the scientific community do.'

'You are the person who confuses metaphysics with another study. You accuse me of turning metaphysics into theology of one kind or another. But you do worse! You degrade it to the level of the special sciences, making it one amongst others. But it precedes them and is naturally superior to them.'

'But did you not believe ten years ago that philosophy was descriptive psychology?'

Devlin examined his *vis-à-vis* with a curious care. 'Are you being disingenuous?' he asked sharply.

'I be disingenuous? Never in your life!'

'Then surely you must understand what Husserl meant when he said that phenomenology was descriptive psychology. He meant that it provided general schemata of the conditions of personal experience. He hoped that it might rescue psychology from bald empiricism ...'

'... which it hasn't,' said Souverain, with a touch of asperity.

'No, it hasn't,' admitted Devlin vigorously, 'and you as an historian should know the reasons for this. The climate doesn't favour general science. And philosophy is the general science, the highest science in the natural order, and not, as you make out, another special science.'

'You transform it into natural theology.'

'I do not!'

'But I see no difference.'

Devlin showed some impatience. 'Natural theology depends on and assumes the natural religious impulse, if not the supernatural. Metaphysics does nothing of the kind, as you very well know.'

'But only you, and others like you, can distinguish them. You understand, I hope, that I am not the enemy of theology, natural or supernatural, but I do not like to see things intermingled which should be kept apart. This is important, is it not?'

'Things should be called by their right names, certainly.'

'Then how does your metaphysics deserve another name than that of natural theology?' Souverain had begun to feel his composure slipping away from him. He had no taste for debates like these and suspected that his position was, in some special hidden way, perfectly false. The man opposite him was a decade his junior and presumably more vigorous. Yet Devlin had somehow made him feel like a suppliant, an aspirant, a young student ignorant of something which he must learn. He moved uneasily in his seat and listened.

'I am moved by an impulse which is not religious, and I see and investigate in a purely human way. My science is inferior to supernatural theology and to natural theology, and superior to every other. Inferior to the theologies because its object is not the Person of the Godhead as such, superior to every other science because possessing as its object the whole of Being instead of some special aspect or parcel of local being. It is true, I suppose, that metaphysics has God, finally, as its highest object; but it is not the science of God either as revealed or as manifested in the natural order. Its object is Being as such, and as it can be known naturally, without requiring any form of religious assent, or even the naturally religious stance and inclination of the feelings.'

'Then anyone can be a metaphysician?'

'Can anyone be an historian like yourself?' He watched Souverain wince. 'Only those who have the gift.'

'Intuitionism!'

'Yes, but not in your bad sense. This is not a matter of esoterica but of high difficult cultivation of the powers of the intellect. And it produces no books and no little articles – because it is the end of research. Possess the intuition of Being and there can be no need to write books. Books of metaphysics are not metaphysics itself but only heuristic devices, prolegomena. The metaphysician who writes books is to that degree the less a metaphysician.'

'I can't admit that. Every other form of knowledge requires communication. Sacred worship requires a community. If your institute communicates nothing to the public, it has no reason for existence as a teaching body.'

'Sacred worship is not the only form of prayer, my friend.'

'No.'

'And the institute is not a teaching body; it is a community of contemplation, but not,' he continued as Souverain began to interrupt, 'not religious contemplation. Pure ontological contemplation. We do not hold conversations, we think together. Books are for conversations: contemplation is not.'

'Such an institute is worthless. To put it in the simplest terms, the governors of the university insist on more frequent publication. That is, results.'

'Ends are worthless,' said Devlin slowly, 'truth is worthless, you can do nothing with it. What can you do with a painting but look at it?' He gazed intently at Souverain. 'You agree with them and come here to discharge me?'

'Not in my own favour.'

'In favour of one of your instruments, that machine, Boscawen.'

'You are too hard on him; you believe that he has betrayed you. He had made a perfectly legitimate choice, and has had the right to do so.'

Devlin began to laugh slowly. 'I'm proud enough to assert that I have no pride of that stripe. Do you follow me? I don't require the headship of any organization. I'm content to be a private professor without any superior place. But I am sorry to see thought supplanted by apparatus.'

Souverain shrugged. 'It is the way things are,' he said.

Devlin laughed louder. 'Metaphysics can see even that.' He was feeling better. 'It can even see the way things are. You may have the institute, my friend, and I will be happy to assist you, or any other of its officers, in anything. And now, if you will excuse me, I believe that I'll go home and rest. I have the habit of lying down for a while in the afternoon.' He rose, and Souverain, who felt that the termination of the interview should have come from him, rose with him and tried to appear as if he had in fact given the *congé*. They walked together to the door of the presidential office, and at the door shook hands.

'You may tell Boscawen,' said Devlin, 'that he has nothing to fear from me. I don't mean to embarrass him. He was one of my first students, you know, though not perhaps one of the very best.'

'He has some capacity,' said Souverain, although he secretly agreed with the estimate.

'Capacity of the fourth or fifth rank, which will suffice. You can announce that my term of office has expired and that I don't wish it renewed for personal reasons. That will not be a lie. I suppose I have no administrative talent but I've been able to see how things were going. Good afternoon, M. Souverain.' He walked quietly downstairs and went home. At the end of the year he took a long vacation from his professorial duties.

No one ever takes a vacation from thought so it is to be supposed that he took his reflections with him wherever he travelled.

In September of 1946 the new administration of the institute was installed, a fine new building begun, young professors engaged, the courses expanded and subtilized, and the original foundation altered out of all recognition except for the presence of Francis X. Devlin on the staff as a senior professor. The transformed school began to wax and grow fat, trebling its enrolment, quintupling its rate of publication. A detached observer might have objected that nothing remained of the original conception of the institute except its name. But the name and the reputation were the great thing. A publishing imprint was established and a line of chastely bound *Studies in Ontology: Series One* began to appear, besides pamphlets, transcriptions of congresses, and various direct-mailing pieces of a promotional nature.

A GREAT TEACHER who writes nothing is left almost without resources in the world of politics and affairs, as the great example of Socrates suggests. Devlin never did anything to proclaim that he was another Socrates; he would have laughed at the notion. But like Socrates he possessed the only (the very great) resource of the teacher, that is, his pupils, a group of men who began in the early nineteen-fifties to emerge from the terrible darkness into which they had marched a decade before. The fifth of those first doctorates, General Boscawen, had prospered. But so had three of the others.

One of them, the existentialist theologian Roscoe Fetzer, now ranked very high at Harvard Divinity.

Another, Dr. Hugh Frazier the psychiatrist, had been on the cover of *Time* and was now a maker of opinion in the left wing of the medical profession, and a frequent consultant to Washington.

The third, the renowned Thomist theorist of the concept, Martin O'Mara, had taken holy orders and was now a *monsignor* and the chancellor of an enormous Catholic university not far from Burlington.

These three disciples, together with a band of younger

Devlinians, were not pleased, not pleased at all, to see their mentor put aside, at the instigation as they believed of a Frenchman, in favour of their old fellow student Boscawen. They formed at first a cabal, and then a visible party, and at last a rather vocal lobby. They were all members of the American Academy of Philosophy by virtue of those ancient earned doctorates, and they positively began to put it about that Francis X. Devlin had been shamefully treated at Burlington.

Msgr O'Mara invited Devlin to come to his university and found a newer, better, more uplifted institute, with a new name and new credentials, but with the old vision and fire.

Roscoe Fetzer put Devlin's name discreetly into circulation at Harvard as a potential University Scholar and the mooting of this appointment, when it came to the ears of the authorities in Burlington, terrified them. They had overlooked these resources of the teacher and were astonished to see them rise up and threaten to overwhelm them. A University Scholar – when they had as good as fired him?

Dr Hugh Frazier roamed further afield and intimated in Washington the propriety of Devlin's nomination as a U.S. Commissioner of Education. And this likelihood too alarmed the resident daimon at Burlington.

Through it all, Frank Devlin maintained a discreet and creditable silence, as was to be expected from so disinterested a thinker. He taught two courses at the institute, offering them in alternate years, hoarding his lecture notes, adding to them always in his tiny, miraculously legible handwriting, deepening them with every new delivery, and amplifying their scope. The course titles perhaps just hint a further resource beyond the loyalty of his old students; they almost seem to imply that he contemplated the ultimate commission of his reflections to the press. For they were called: '*The Ego and the Problem of Freedom*' and '*Concept and Essence: Towards a Realist Epistemology*'.

Every time General Boscawen looked at those titles, as he examined the institute's catalogue, he felt a shiver run up his spine as though, in the popular phrase, someone were walking on his grave. They looked so like the titles of books and, as it might be, renowned important books. Then he would reflect that Devlin just couldn't do a thing like that, not holding the opinions he did about publication, and he was right. Devlin never did.

By the time he was sixty, in 1955, it had become evident to his party, his friends and the new young men of the postwar generation who knew him by his vast reputation, and by the sinister stories circulated about the conduct of his opponents, that he himself would never write up these valuable reflections. They thought about the two courses, with the two wonderful titles. And then they always thought about Lord Acton and shuddered. It was obvious that the fruits of their master's entire career as a thinker could not be allowed to die with him; the generations had passed so quickly and he who had been the young and vigorous leader of the philosophic revolt of a generation ago was now approaching retirement and silence. There was no time to lose.

His friends did what Acton's should have done. They hired an amanuensis, a professional shorthand reporter, much as Aristotle's admirers must have done (for only on some such supposition can the condition of the *Metaphysics* be explained) and paid his tuition as a graduate student at the institute. In the natural order of things he attended Devlin's final course offerings just before his retirement, in the academic years 1960-61 and 1961-62. They did not attempt to conceal this stratagem, being honourable men and philosophers, but they didn't broadcast it either. Only last spring did it become a matter of common knowledge that these lecture notes had been taken down precisely as delivered, and that so far as could be known they were long enough to form two major publications.

By then it was too late for the authorities at the University of Burlington to do anything but get in line behind the other groups of the philosopher's friends who wished to obtain permission to edit and publish his manuscripts. He listened with his invariable courtesy to every emissary who came seeking such permission but insisted on reserving the disposition of the rights to his writings until after he retired when he would have the chance to assess his situation. In June of last year he retired, laden with the praises, the encomiums, of the entire world of professional philosophy. Even the seventy-five-year-old Amédée Souverain, who spoke to no one these days because he was so taken up with his projected work on art history, even Souverain came forward with a testimonial in print. It was the pinnacle of Devlin's career. His last professional action was his attendance at the annual meeting of the American Academy of Philosophy, for 1962, held last December in Milwaukee.

Frazier, Fetzer, Msgr O'Mara, their host of friends, and their chief had dined long and well on the evening of the first day's proceedings, almost too well in fact, so that when Frank Devlin got to his feet and spoke, rather indistinctly, of his feelings on the occasion of this formal leavetaking, a very young member of the gathering felt impelled to ask his neighbour what he thought of the philosopher's condition.

'Can he be drunk?' asked the young man nervously, and his neighbour stared at him distantly.

'Francis Devlin drunk? In the twenty years I've known him, he's never taken so much as a glass of wine. I imagine it's his feelings.'

'Come on up to my room,' Devlin kept saying, 'Come on up, and I'll tell you all about that shrimp Boscawen.' He sat down abruptly and looked disconsolately around as the dinner party broke up. A few of his oldest friends escorted him upstairs.

Sitting on the edge of the bed in his shirt and suspenders, nodding his head at his students he seemed very old and suddenly very human, more like themselves than he'd ever seemed before. 'The university is the character,' he said several times, 'the university is the person. I never understood before how an institution might have a life of its own like a human life. Cardinal Newman once suggested that a mob had an individual daimonic personality, larger than the persons who individually composed it. Perhaps the university does too, perhaps it has an indwelling guardian.' He let himself loll sideways onto his bed and in a minute was fast asleep. Dr Frazier and Msgr O'Mara studied his face as they adjusted him on the bed, drawing off his clothes and making him comfortable for the long night.

'He had nothing to drink,' said Frazier dolefully.

'He's getting old,' said the Monsignor. 'I never knew a man to go downhill so fast.'

They tiptoed to the door, leaving the master to his rest.

Since his death at Christmas, the testamentary dispositions of the philosopher have become public property. He assigned to his personal literary executors, Frazier, Fetzer and O'Mara, the publication rights to his later manuscripts, including the celebrated lecture notes. The world of scholarship looks forward hourly to their appearance. The executors have chosen an expert editor and arranged for publication with the most distinguished and venerable of university presses. The philosophic community expects two fat volumes, carefully annotated and explicated, with facsimile reproductions of Devlin's handwriting in the crucial places. No one can remember when the announcement of two forthcoming volumes has excited such comment. Through the scholarly grapevine one hears that our expectations will be in no wise disappointed.

And to the University of Burlington he left, in the actual words of his testament: 'All rights in the writings which were the fruits of my earlier years, that is: My first book, on Brentano, my two articles in German in the *Jahrbuch,* my two book reviews, in *Philosophy* and *Phenomenological Research,* and my correspondence until December 31st, 1939.' It was apparently his intention to divide the responsibilities of publication systematically.

It must be noted that the University of Burlington has lost no time in making available the documents assigned to its care. On February 15th of this year there appeared the 'Collected Papers, of Francis X. Devlin' as the initial volume in *Studies in Ontology: Series Two.* On the title page of the handsomely produced book there appears as an epigraph the aphorism which was rarely out of Devlin's thoughts in his last years. 'The university is the person.'

'And after all,' as the newly installed young Dean of the faculty of graduate studies remarked, 'though it hardly comes to three hundred pages, after all, it's a book, it's on the record now. It's a publication.'

Suites and Single Rooms, with Bath

LOOK AT ME, how did I get *here*? Everything was so solid and permanent, nothing could break it, we were set for life. I don't know how the change began, how what we were grew into what we are. I can't remember what we did wrong, and especially what I did wrong. But Christ, I'm an adult, I know I did something and kept on doing it for a long time, because only five years ago my wife loved me with an inexhaustible love. I could do anything, say anything, do *things* to her like telling her she had no talent and was kidding herself. You can only say those things to somebody you can trust not to hit back.

Where were we at the start, the first year? It's hard to remember, what I can't figure out is how you could get from there to here, she despises me, she can't stand to be in a room with me. I wouldn't have believed she could get to that point; there was no signal, no place where we might have stopped, where I might have said to myself this far but no farther, if you say that, it'll ruin everything.

I kept being able to pull things back together after every fight, hell, everybody fights, you can hear them through the walls. A fight is just an aphrodisiac, any nickel-and-dime psychologist will tell you that. I'm just a *Ladies Home Journal* cliché. 'Can this marriage be saved?' No, it can't.

We used to read those things about Joe the big Swede and Mary the pretty high-school teacher, making eight hundred a month between them. Joe hated Mary because she didn't shave her legs, and Mary hated Joe because he spoke poor English. Then Dr. Popenoe would tell Mary to use Gillette, just like Zsa Zsa, and he would tell Joe to read a grammar book and *presto* they were deeply in love all over again.

That isn't how it is. I wonder why I don't have any feelings. I used to say, 'I have feelings. I'm really sorry I said that, just remember I'm not made of lead. I have feelings, you know.' But I didn't and I don't now. She has the children and naturally, the way things are, they're going to love her and hate me. I don't mind. I don't feel anything about that, you have to write these things off. There's a certain amount that happens to you that you have to write off and forget. The kids are gone, OK, I'll get more. What's a kid or two?

If anybody heard me say that out loud, the men in the white coats would be along. It's funny what you can get away with, if you keep it to yourself. Unspeakable things. You're all right as long as you don't say them. Remember the time she threw the milk-bottle and it just missed my ear. She threw to miss; if she'd hit me, she'd have skulled me. It made that little round hole in the plaster and when the kids asked what it was, we told them it was a door for the mice. They kept calling down the hole, for the mice to come out and play. A perfect circle about the size of a silver dollar like she'd done it with a cookie-cutter. I can think of lots of unspeakable things to say, but it makes me wonder if I'm not a little bit unbalanced. I think I've got it under control, people don't seem to suspect, but I just don't *mind*. I should mind. I know I should be devastated about the children but the truth is, they were a hell of a nuisance. I don't think the baby stopped crying twice the first year.

You can take just so much of that. My little girl insisted on sitting on the arm of my chair while I was reading the morning paper. Now I ask you, how can you tell that to a judge? What's he going to think, if you tell him, 'Jesus, Judge, I could have killed that kid, she wouldn't leave me alone.' You know what he's going to say to that, don't you? Sure! He's going to say you're a monster without the basic human affections; if you ever told a judge that, he'd lock you up.

No, I don't think he'd have the power. You can't convict yourself out of your own mouth. Besides everybody feels like that sometimes; they just don't admit it to themselves. She was nice enough sometimes; it made me feel pretty good to watch her when she was asleep. Ha ha ha (very cynical) that's the best time with kids, when they're asleep and not making a lot of goddamn noise. How I hate noise! It was mainly the noise that did it, noise noise noise until I found myself shaking all the time I was home. When you have to get out of the house and go to work to stop shaking, there's something radically wrong. I mean your house is supposed to be peaceful.

That's one thing about this room, it's quiet, even though I'm in the middle of the city. I get a kick out of lying here with the lights out, listening to the cars go by outside. The curtains muffle everything. And later on, after midnight, it's so quiet I love it, boy, there's nothing like quietness to stop the shakes. Oh that noise, it was driving me out of my mind, I tell you.

Comfortable bed, too. I'm as comfortable here as I ever was in the apartment, just like I told her. It isn't a small room either; it's plenty big enough for a bedroom and living room and it's all mine without the rocking horse and the tricycles. I know where everything is, which I never did before, peace, thank God, peace. This is a nice room, just like I told her.

'Don't you bother your curly head about me, lover. For three hundred a month I could live like a king, if I had my books and records.'

'Take your stinking books and records, they're the only thing you'll spend a cent on. Nobody gets to read them but you.'

'If you weren't so stupid, sweetie, you'd read a book now and then, you haven't opened one since we were married. The only reason you ever read any books was to persuade some unfortunate man that you had the rudiments of an education. I don't know how I fell for it.'

'You never shut up long enough to think about it.'

'You were happy enough to listen to me, the places I took you.'

'Ha! The last time we saw a play was on our honeymoon.'

'Oh oh oh he never takes me anywhere. Go on, now you're supposed to say "I haven't a thing to wear."'

'You said it, I didn't. That's your guilty conscience.'

'*My guilty conscience?* What have I got to be guilty about? I'm not guilty of anything, don't try to hang anything on me.'

'You're the one who said it, and you're right. I haven't bought a thing since we were married, my panties are all held up with pins.'

'It's nice something's holding them up.'

'What do you mean by that, you little prick? When would I ever see another man? Holding my pants up, goddamn you, if I ever get out of this I'll stay so far away from men I'll forget what they look like, all except you. I'm afraid I'll remember you.'

'We can't get out. We're stuck!'

'The kids would be glad if we broke up; they hate it here.'

That was the first time she dared to take me up on it, and once she'd done that, the whole business was over. I never thought she'd ever take me seriously, I guess I said it once too often, ha ha ha the joke's on me, it really is, I said it once too often.

It isn't the end of everything. I'm still young enough to get married again, but after this I don't think I'll ever want to. I mean I've got this nice room, no kids around, look what I've got! I can give her two-thirds of my salary and still live good. (It's too much, I'll cut it down, why should I be noble when it isn't in the agreement, it costs a man as much to live as it does a woman and two kids, she doesn't need to keep up appearances.)

I need two new suits, I could live like a king on three hundred a month net, but she gets twice that and she buys ballet lessons for God's sake. Why should they have ballet lessons when I need two new suits? If I don't look good at work, the money stops coming. They might as well not be my children, I never get to see them, not that I specially want to because pretty soon they won't be mine. I don't see how a woman can do that, make children hate their father, but that's what she's doing. So why worry? I can't change it, so why fight it? In five years they won't remember me.

By that time I'll have children of my own and she can find some other sucker to pay for ballet lessons. It works both ways; she'll have as hard a time getting used to it as me. Harder. She's still got the kids around her neck, whereas I've got a comfortable place to live, and all my books and records.

Ho ho ho I'll bet she's glad to have the books out of there, they must have embarrassed her – she never read one of them. I think the bitch is functionally illiterate; she could read the labels in the supermarket and that's about all, and she sure as hell couldn't read price tags.

'How dare you reproach me about money? Any other woman in our circumstances would spend twice what I do.'

'Yeah? How is it that the norm for a family of four is twenty-eight dollars a week for groceries?'

'Is that in the paper? Let me see that! Oh sure, that's a slob's budget. Do you want to eat like a busboy or a construction worker? You're the one who wants porterhouse every night, and whipping cream on your cereal. You're the one who won't let me use powdered milk or margarine because they don't taste right and you're the one who says that a cheap cut of beef is uneatable. If I bring shoulder of beef into the house I get the hurt little boy look. *That's* how you feed a family of four on twenty-eight dollars a week, you eat liver (and liver isn't cheap either) and stew and braised shoulder of beef.'

'We economize on me to begin with! Why always me? Why do you have to have seventeen bottles of cleansing cream? You're not *that* dirty.'

'Funny, funny, oh, you're so funny.'

I don't understand how we got around to talking like that, I really don't. We're the same age, we like the same things, we had children and they're supposed to hold you together. I don't get it.

I ought to get off this bed. I shouldn't lie around like this, it's probably bad for me. I should be out meeting people somewhere. Where? I should get around and go bowling or something. Let me see? Who do I know that I could go and see, that isn't married? I can't go near anybody that's married, at least for a year or two, the way they look at you, you'd think it was catching, that you caught it like you do measles, so they don't want me around. Who could I go and see?

It's funny to have to think about it at all. Six years ago I would simply walk along the street and go into a bar, and there would always be lots of people I knew. Now when I go into a bar I sit there alone for two hours, while a lot of young punks think about making pickups and never get up their courage. A sad sight. A sad sight. I guess we were young punks six years ago, and I guess we looked just as pimply to all those guys who were sitting by themselves, waiting for somebody to join them.

I used to wonder why they sat alone. Now I know.

IT WAS A STRETCHED-OUT suite of rooms in a row from infra-rub to ultraviolate, and beyond that white. Not just seven rooms, a number you couldn't guess, like a long hotel. At first you were in a room well below red, a fixed static colour, the furniture low red, the walls the same and the pictures on the walls, you wore red glasses, the whole bath of colour heating and feeding, the blood-consciousness, the warm dark red, married and secure, loved as a husband, revered as a kind father, and imperceptibly the feeling-tone, the colour, began to change.

It wasn't the walls that changed, they stayed smooth and oblong, you passed from one room to the next and the next and so on but you weren't conscious of passing. The colour swam from infra-red to red and on upwards through the spectrum, like a warm bath that gradually becomes boiling. One chose to walk, the second room was not the first, nor the second the third. There was a series of places, blue places, yellow places, and the shades between. You moved and yet you didn't, you wanted to get out and you couldn't. The sense of fluid change and the sense of the static box, the trap. The colours went on changing upwards but you walked willingly from one room to the next, unconscious of the walk, doors opened by themselves. They flew open as you came along, who opened them? She didn't, one's heart, one's wife, she was in a room beyond and there was no catching her but the doors flew open and the day grew ever sunnier, one merged into violet to ultraviolate past the final near off-white as the sun refuses to appear, hiding behind the smooth ceiling of cloud and here I am walking into daylight, full day, whiteness, this illusory blank freedom.

Where did that come from?

It isn't good to go on lying here, I've been doing it too long, it grows on you. I shouldn't have the lights turned off, I ought to read something or play a record. I know what I ought to do. I ought to take a course at the university, maybe get my master's. I'd meet people that way. There must be a lot of them trying to improve themselves, for God's sake. And there are the girls in the office, they come and go and some of them aren't too bad. There's that Lisa, boy, like a snake, just like a snake. I don't know how she gets into those skirts – with a shoehorn maybe, or maybe she greases herself and slides in.

I'll drive myself nuts if I go on thinking this way. What time is it? Nine-fifteen, getting late, I'll have to decide if I want to get up and go some place. Six years ago I'd be putting on a clean starched white shirt, knotting a regimental tie, going down to watch television, and we'd go somewhere after and stay up till three. None of them do that any more, and those who do are starting to call me Mister. What'll I do, take a book and go up the New Idea Lunch for a milkshake? A big time. Boy!

I'll just lie here a minute longer and think about it.

Jesus, I don't want to think about it.

They're all gone, all married, the only guy that isn't married is queer. I can't get mixed up with Jakie, there's nothing in the queer bars for me.

When I go back to the old places the waiters look sorry for me. I'm bitched, I'm bitched.

No, I'm not. I can think and I can plan, I'll sign up for courses at the university this fall. Half the classes will be girls. They may all be unattractive mice with glasses but they'll have friends, they're bound to. And some of these friends will be worth looking at. I'll cut my support payments; they're bigger than they have to be legally. I should never have started that but I didn't know what I was doing. Then I'll buy those new suits, I'll start looking after my clothes. I'll arrange to have enough money to live in decent style; maybe I'll get a little apartment where I can have people in. One room is no good for that, they get to feeling sorry for you. I'll wipe out the last five years and take up where I left off. I'll take it fairly easy around the office so I'll have energy for school. Maybe I'll take some courses in drama or art or journalism, so I'll meet some interesting people. They may guess I'm older than they are but they don't have to know for sure, and it'll make me more interesting, somebody who's been around.

I'll get in with the Stanley Street crowd, and they don't need to know anything about it at the office. I'll have a ball.

And she won't. She can't get out of the apartment; she can't get another man very easily, not with two kids. If it weren't for her mother, she'd never get out at all. I hope I don't get to meeting her in the Stanley Street places. I don't want her telling people about me. That's the only trouble with the whole bit – they know so much about you. Sure, I did some bastardly things, and maybe I've got some funny ideas about sex, but so has she, so has she, brother, and just let her start telling tales, just let her make *move one,* boy, and I'll let them know about some of the positions she liked and that'll be that. She'd better not fool around with me because I know just as much about her. More. But I hope I don't meet her anywhere when I'm with a girl.

I'll get myself a car, a European car, they look quite sporty and don't cost too much. Perhaps I'll get a Karmann-Ghia; it isn't a sports car but it looks sharp and most people don't know the difference. I'll roll around, here and there, hither and yon, and I'll make out. I'll get some dishes and stuff and eat at home, when I've got my apartment. I can have a steak dinner at home for half what it costs me in the New Idea Lunch or some other cruddy place. I'll have beer parties, and then I've got custody of the records, thank God, they make all the difference to a party. I'll get some bullfight posters with my own name on them, and that and change the place around.

Nine-thirty. If I lie here much longer I'll fall asleep. A bad bad sign when you start falling asleep at home on Friday night, you're having the male menopause, boy, you're getting to be a lonely old man.

I'm no lonely old man, I'm thirty. I've got forty years to go, perhaps longer, I'm in good shape. My life isn't over just because I made one mistake. You read all these magazine articles like that series in *Life,* and they contradict themselves. They say either a divorced man can never have a good marriage, or he'll be more careful the second time and have a wonderful marriage. So which is it? I know I won't make the same mistake again, but I might make a different mistake. It's like tuberculosis, you carry the seeds around inside you and you never suspect they're there.

They say you have a tendency to marry the same type of

person, same looks, same habits, that would be awful, I'll have to watch out for that. If I couldn't make it with her, I'll never make it with some carbon copy. I'll watch out for blonde girls, big girls, girls who had careers, only children, girls who watch their figures, girls who want a lot of children. Do I have to avoid the whole syndrome, or each individual characteristic? Could I marry a blonde girl who was one of ten children and who hated kids? Or are blondes poison for me? How can you ever tell?

Then there are all the things that were wrong with me, that I've got to be afraid of. I was irresponsible, so I'll have to be responsible. I was spending too much dough, so I'll be a goddamn miser. I stayed home nights; I'll start running around.

There are so many things to think about that you can't cover them all, you can't protect yourself in the clinches. If I could afford it, I'd get some counselling, but I can't do that and rent an apartment and buy a Karmann-Ghia. The counselling should come first, I know, I know, but I've only got one life, and I can't get rid of every pleasure just to be *healthy*.

I can't remember how we got started. I've blocked it out, I guess, but it was somewhere in the third year, somewhere in through there, the first year was fine, no sweat, no stress, like the time we drove to New York for Thanksgiving, we were on the parkway for six hours on account of the holiday traffic, and neither of us got mad, we sang all the way in, we listened to the radio and sang, having a fine time. We were going to go straight to bed when we got in, but the trip took longer and longer, instead of an hour and a half it took six. It was three o'clock when we made the hotel, and when we got into bed we both fell asleep.

In the morning we made love while we were waiting for room service, it had a kind of exhibitionistic quality, I guess, because he could have walked in on us, right in the act. I don't believe either of us would have turned a hair, we were married after all, and everybody knows married people share the same bed. We just went on lying there, watching daytime TV, which we never did at home, and every now and then we'd have another cup of coffee – room service had to come back twice with coffee – the waiter must have thought we were some kind of sexual gymnasts. He couldn't understand why we wouldn't get out of bed.

'Do you suppose he thinks we aren't married?'

'Christ, no! If we weren't, we'd be sitting across the room from each other. These guys learn to judge people, and it isn't that kind of hotel.'

'I'll put my black bra and pants on, and give him something to think about.' She made me laugh; they always want to act like whores, as long as nobody thinks that's what they are.

'Leave them off!'

'What?'

'I said leave them off!'

'You sound like Alan Ladd. That's an Alan Ladd line; they never gave him more than five words in a row.' But she left them off and I got a big charge out of her walking around the room naked for the rest of the morning. She never would at home but she didn't seem to mind in unfamiliar circumstances. When the waiter came back for the cart she had to hide in the bathroom, I had to laugh.

We were fine then and the next year we had the baby and we never got back to the city. We both swore that we'd never pay money for baby-sitters and we never did, so we never got out. That wasn't a good move; perhaps if I'd spent a few dollars on sitters I wouldn't be here.

But I want to be here; I don't want to be back in the apartment.

But I didn't then.

You figure it out; it's too much for me, now I want to but I didn't then. I wanted to a year ago, which leaves a three-year gap, it got started somewhere in there, can I get a better fix on it? For the year after the baby came we were all right, we had a lot of fun with her and we conceived the second one in a walk, home and cooled out, and then things began to change.

I remember thinking, just before the second one arrived, that it might help us get along better. *That's* where it was, in there somewhere towards the end of the third year, and from there it was a fast two years to where we are now. Free. Yes, sir, we've got our freedom, and isn't it nice just a nice bright day and you can't see the sun because it's gone behind the clouds and the whole sky seems white, an undivided white, we're free, like coming out of a long tunnel, a long straight suite of rooms in a honeymoon hotel starting with the infra-red warm and dark, we made love on the bathroom floor in that hotel, the steam made the tiles warm and wet, and after that things began to be brighter and brighter, our blue days, our yellow days.

It's all fantasy, there's just no way.

Quarter to ten.

I can't lie here all night, I'll never get to sleep if I do. I'll get up and go out, put on my clean shirt and my striped tie, take a little money from the drawer, get along, get along. I'll make new friends in the bars. I'll get girls.

Getting on for ten. Ah! It's too late, there's no reason to go out. I've got to get up and get my clothes on and get out of here because if I don't I'm afraid I'll never go out again.

The Ingenue I Should Have Kissed, but Didn't

NOW IT'S SPRING and the voice of the actor is heard in the land. Here in Montreal, French companies are rehearsing Molière, Ghelderode, Tardieu; the English prepare the lesser works of Molnar, and across the nation arrangements for the Dominion Drama Festival go forward as merry as a marriage bell, and in some cases merrier.

I was once an actor myself. Once and once only I trod the boards of the Royal Alexandra, in the finals of the festival in the spring of 1949 when I took a minor but calamitous part in a production of *Another Part of the Forest* which won the regional run-off but lost out in the finals to a Hamilton production of *John Loves Mary.* My acting career was in fact disastrous for almost every one of the two dozen plays I appeared in; but disaster or none, I had the hell of a fine time in this theatre or that. I learned a lot and I've never been able to forget the days when I was maybe the worst actor in Toronto.

I was all right as long as I had nothing to do. I could even read lines if nobody was paying any attention to me, and my first role was exactly suited to my limited talents. I played Father Time in a one-acter that Saint Michael's College entered in the All-Varsity Drama Festival. I sat at a table, way over stage left on the apron, and read two very long, dull, quasi-philosophical speeches between the scenes. I had an hour-glass in front of me which half-hid me from view, and I sustained these two meditations apparently quite acceptably. I had a curious makeup, almost a disguise, in that part, which I'd devised myself. My hair was full of white stick; it was so tacky that I looked like I'd been cast in plaster and I'd so lined my face as to suggest a species of mummification. They took photographs of the show, including one of me crouching defensively behind my hourglass. Later on when I was proudly showing a print to some friends of the family, one of them said off the end of her tongue: 'Is that your grandmother?' She meant it quite innocently, but I felt a certain chagrin and stopped exhibiting the picture, though I believe my mother still has it somewhere.

That was the winter of my freshman year, and I was hooked, good and hooked, on acting, and so kept at it for close to five years, though I soon realized that I'd never be any good. There were many extremely talented people around the university at that time, and they set a demanding standard.

At the end of that season I heard that Mr Gill was casting what became the first of his annual Shakespearian productions, *Romeo and Juliet*. The principal roles were cast by the time I plucked up enough courage to go around to the office in Hart House Theatre, but I did manage to get my name on a list of extra ladies and gentlemen, and was present at the last ten days of the meticulous rehearsals for which Bob Gill became known and respected. He blocked the crowd scenes with even greater care than those of the principals, giving each of us a character to assume. One lad was to be an old vendor of cakes, another was a cutpurse (there's a cutpurse in everything by Shakespeare), and I and a young girl from the art college were a pair of child lovers, and we looked pretty young at that.

All the principals had brand-new costumes. I can remember Charm King's and Murray Davis's vividly, hers virginal white, his silver and blue, and I've since seen those costumes in a hundred pieces on CBC-TV and elsewhere. I drew one of Malabar's vintage numbers, a green affair with inhibiting tights, and a floppy motheaten hat with a ribboned tail to it.

Bob Gill took one look at me, smothered a laugh, and said: 'Keep it, Hugh! It's period.'

Henry Kaplan, who was not in the show but was sitting in to observe Bob's directorial methods, remembered me from my first efforts and said expansively: 'I know you. You were pretty good in *Lucifer at Large*.' That was the name of the piece in which I had played Father Time. I didn't disillusion Henry, and later on he had cause to regret the accuracy of his memory. But he was always polite and helpful to me, Henry was, and these days he's right up there with the good ones.

The Globe and Mail gave *Romeo and Juliet* an ecstatic notice, and Toronto theatre-goers at once decided that a Shakespearian production should conclude each Hart House season, the student theatre being considered fully and solidly launched. But despite their on-campus celebrity, there were several young actors and actresses who wanted to try something on their own, free of Bob Gill's tutelage and under the direction of a man their own age – a natural feeling in no way reflecting on Bob who was wise enough then and later to encourage it. What was wanted was money, first of all, and then a place to mount a production, and the obvious place was the Central Ontario Drama Festival.

So early in 1949 that nice girl Isobel Manners organized a group called the Actor's Workshop or the Players' Studio or some such name – I don't remember offhand – to enter a piece in the festival under the direction of Henry Kaplan. I'm not certain, but I believe that this was one of the first things Henry staged for a Toronto audience, though he was recognized from his work with the Straw Hat Players as a coming director with methods of his own. He relied much more on the actor's inner intuitions than Bob Gill did, sometimes with striking results. He and Isobel put their heads together and chose a play, Lillian Hellman's *Another Part of the Forest,* not perhaps the best conceivable choice for a fledgling company, though it's hard to say what else they might have chosen.

Some said that Isobel had sold her pearls to back the show, which may not have been true but which makes a fine story. She and Henry assembled an all-star line-up for the principal roles, six of whom became highly competent professionals: Eric House, Ted Follows, Bill Hutt, Bea Lennard, Isobel herself, and the ingenue Betty Reilly. And Henry of course became a professional director. There was also a girl in the cast named Clarine Jackman, very strong, a very big quality, who played the slightly crazy mother in the Hellman play. I've often wondered what happened to her – she was a very promising actress indeed. Also in a principal role was John Walker, for many years with CBC Radio and now a professor of French at the University of Toronto, a noted *seiziémiste* and a big D'Aubigné man. And there was me.

One February morning Clarine came to me in the hall after a

lecture at Saint Mike's and said: 'How would you like to take a small part in a play off-campus?' I can remember my answer verbatim.

'Why don't they get somebody who can act?'

Clarine acknowledged the perfect justice of the question but said that it would be good training for me and might reveal hitherto unsuspected gifts (a beguiling argument), and anyway I was curious about some of the people whose names she mentioned, which made me decide to have a go. She told me that the rehearsals were at Isobel Manners' home, gave me the address, and told me to came along next Wednesday night. I was flattered to be asked because everybody knew that these were the best actors on the campus and maybe in all of Toronto. All except Betty Reilly – I'd never heard of her and she wasn't then identified with Hart House.

The Manners house was rather daunting, an enormous place with a conservatory and a sunken garden, up in Forest Hill. Later on I heard a funny story about that house and about a party held there to celebrate the birth of a wonderful new literary magazine. It really *was* a wonderful magazine as a matter of fact – the three issues that actually appeared are now collectors' items – but it died speedily. It must have cost the earth to produce. Anyway there was this party where the guests were wandering all over the house, getting lost, looking for secret passages, playing hide-and-seek and generally carrying on in very high spirits.

As I heard it, one of them wandered into an untenanted bedroom *and fell downstairs in it,* the only Toronto house I can think of where you can fall downstairs in a bedroom. I guess there are others now, there's a lot of new money in town, but I don't know about them. A butler came with the Manners house, and a staff, and all together it was quite something.

Wednesday night I turned up at the door and the butler helped me off with my coat, mistaking my profound silence for assurance, or so I hoped, and said sepulchrally, 'Miss Isobel and the company are in the rehearsal hall, sir.' I nodded, secretly unnerved. He didn't have to tell *me* where to find it, and after some time I located it in the cellar. Betty Reilly was reading through her most important scene and now I could see why she was in the company: she was a fireball, a hot property, a talent, even then you could see it – she was a natural. I wondered why she hadn't been working at Hart House, and somebody told me that she studied with Mr Sterndale Bennett at the Conservatory and would be appearing in two plays at the Festival, the Conservatory's and our own.

In a few minutes Henry called my little scene, and as I had my ten lines down cold we were able to block it and get it out of the way that night. I could always remember lines effortlessly; that was all I could do with them. It was touch and go whether lines would come out of my mouth or a terrified 'gug gug gug'.

I was supposed to impersonate an old Southern colonel! The scene was mostly with Eric House, playing the domineering father, and Ted Follows, playing his second, or degenerate and worthless, son. When it was over there ensued a stunned silence, as of hard second thoughts, and I sat down. In a few seconds Eric came up to me courteously and said, 'I like your Isham.' Isham was the name of my colonel. I've often wondered since why he was so polite – gratuitous courtesy has always attracted me fatally. Those few words really put me at ease and afterwards I wasn't quite so bad. I've never forgotten that.

I watched a couple of other scenes and then went upstairs and had a beer in the music room. Paid for out of Isobel's pearl-money? I don't know but I enjoyed it. The conservatory led off the music room and John Walker was sitting in there reading and looking saturnine and preoccupied. I didn't join him. Later on he was cast as Cassius, so you can see how I would have felt. In a minute Betty Reilly came into the room, picked up some cheese and crackers, and sat down on the sofa beside me, at once asking me a lot of questions very interestedly. I couldn't understand why. Maybe she had me figured for a hidden talent, like Clarine – I don't know. It seemed to me that she acted odd, and then she was a year or two younger than I, practically a child.

'What's your name, where do you go to school, do you want to act, isn't Eric *so* good, isn't Isobel a peach?' She went on and on, fixing me with huge disturbing eyes.

I edged uneasily an inch or two further down the sofa, wondering what to make of this, while swallowing the last of my beer.

'If you're getting another, would you get one for me?'

'Sure,' I said. I opened two bottles, picked up a second glass, and went back to the sofa. As I handed her the drink she gave me a brilliant smile and patted the cushion beside her.

'You haven't told me a thing about yourself,' she pouted.

I sat down close to her. I was beginning to think she had me mixed up with somebody else. 'I don't know,' I mumbled stupidly. 'I only came because they asked me to.'

'Oh, but you were so *right*, so essentially *right*, to come,' she said. 'One makes these decisions almost intuitively, doesn't one? Or do you feel that way? I mean about what one really demands of life!'

That sounds ridiculous as I put it down, but she had the damnedest way of making these things sound like perfectly ordinary good sense. I don't mean to imply that she was like most actresses, always talking lines, lines, offstage or on. I once met a girl in a bar, a beginning actress, who fixed me with a nasty glare and said: 'I am going to be a great, great star.' But Betty always tried to talk straight when she was off.

She took an outsized swallow of beer, choked slightly, and turned sidewise on the sofa, facing me. I put my glass nervously to my lips. Then she suddenly projected her face forward until it almost collided with mine. I could hear my teeth clinking on the edge of the glass.

'At our age there is so much, so very much, that's still to be discovered,' she announced in low thrilling tones, 'isn't there?'

'Yeah,' I said, 'you're right. There sure is.'

She kept her face flat against mine, our noses nearly bumping like Eskimos, for perhaps thirty seconds, and then she began, slowly at first, to laugh desperately, or in what she thought sounded like a desperate laugh. It certainly convinced me. Then she rose and flounced out of the room, holding the edge of her skirt in the fingers of one hand like a Swedish folk-dancer.

From the conservatory there came a lot of chuckling which irritated me profoundly. I put my head into the room, and there was John Walker looking more saturnine than ever.

'Did you hear all that?' I demanded.

'Yes.'

'Well, what the hell was it all about?'

'It's not for me to say, you understand,' said John, 'but if you ask me, Betty was making a pass at you.'

'At me?'

'Certainly, at you. You were alone with her, weren't you?'

'Yes, but I just thought she was acting a bit odd. Why me?'

'I don't expect it was anything personal,' he said dryly. 'Betty's just growing up, that's all. If it hadn't been you it might have been me, or whoever was in the room, or a soliloquy.'

'You don't mean that she wasn't *sincere*?' At that time I had the notion that I valued sincerity above every other human quality.

'She's always sincere,' he said laughing.

'Then how could it have been you, or nobody, as well as me?'

'I can't explain it,' he said, and just then there came a shout from downstairs for the cast to assemble for a first run-through. The incident stuck in my mind.

The Players' Workshop rehearsed *Another Part of the Forest* for eight weeks, and when it came time to compete in the regional Festival we were honed to a fine edge. That is, everybody else was honed to a fine edge but I remained obdurately at the level of incapacity at which I'd begun. Poor Henry Kaplan, who wanted every part of the show to be as smooth and polished as every other, worked and sweated over my scene until he was forced to confess himself licked. He threatened me, ridiculed me, got mad at me. Once he even shed a few tears and entreated me to remember the reputation of his family. What they had to do with it, I do not know. Nothing he could do would make me a good or even acceptable performer.

'I don't understand you, Hugh,' Henry would cry. 'You're intelligent, you know your lines, you work hard, and when you get onstage something horrible happens to you. You turn into a robot. I don't know what to say to you.' I disturbed Henry very much, but to his great credit he never considered asking me to leave the show. Until, that is, until we won the regional festival and began to be touted as contenders in the Dominion final.

'Look, Henry,' I said to him one afternoon just before the week of the final, 'why don't you replace me? Why not ask Don Davis or somebody to do it as a favour?'

'I've thought of it,' he said glumly, 'I've even asked around. But just about everybody is tied up in Shakespeare with Bob, and then, oh hell, you've been with us from the beginning....' Then he brightened up a bit. 'I'll tell you what we're going to do, we'll get Jack Medhurst in.' Jack Medhurst was Toronto's greatest expert in stage makeup. 'We'll have him do your makeup,' said Henry, 'and, by God, you may not be able to act it, but at least you'll look it!

The day before our performance in the final was, as it happened, my twenty-first birthday. I spent the day getting a card-sized birth certificate at the Parliament Buildings so I could sit in the Chez Paree with a clear conscience, and that night each of the four male members of the cast bought me a birthday drink, four double Scotches, plus the birthday drinks I bought for myself. On the day of the performance I accordingly felt very relaxed, or at least my mind wasn't on my acting. Jack Medhurst did a superlative job on me which was complemented by hangover – I really did look seventy-five, but it was no use. Despite first-class performances from the rest of our cast, the adjudicator didn't care for Lillian Hellman, and we lost the award to Hamilton.

There was some grumbling in the Toronto press on Monday, but the cast took it pretty well. Nobody quit the theatre in disgust, even me. And though by this time my limitations were understood by all, I was allowed to continue taking small parts here and there, in obscure situations where I couldn't mar the general effect, like the crowd scenes, say, in *Julius Caesar*.

I've already mentioned that John Walker was Cassius. Eric House made a superb Casca. Donald Davis was an upright, dignified, and beautifully spoken Brutus. David Gardner, now a producer of drama on CBC-TV, played Mark Antony, and Bill Hutt was Caesar and, later in the play, an impressive ghost.

I played Popilius Lena. If you consult your high-school text of the play you will find that Popilius Lena has one line in the scene at the Forum just before the plotters murder Caesar. The line is as follows:

I wish your enterprise today may thrive.

As Bob Gill interpreted this, it's a wonderful bit of Shakespearian irony. We are not told whether Popilius Lena is aware of the conspiracy; maybe he only refers to Brutus's plea for Metellus Cimber's life and estates. Who knows? In any case, Bob maintained, here's a chance for a bit actor to make a fine impression with this ambiguous and obscure line.

'It's only one line, Hugh,' he would say, 'but it's strong. STRONG.'

Bill Hutt had become a good friend of mine, and he was determined that I should shine in this part. I don't know why, but I seem to have presented some kind of challenge to people like Bill and Henry who thought seriously about character and action. People who had read *An Actor Prepares* and who took the problems of building a performance somewhat to heart. Bill swore that he would polish my performance in that part until I was good.

'You've got it in you,' he would say. 'I'm sure it's there. All we have to do is get it out of you.' But I defied him: he couldn't get it out. He made me read that damned line in every conceivable way, with every possible shift of emphasis, nuance, and attitude. I would come on briskly, and half-shout:

'I wish your *enterprise today* may thrive.'

'Wrong,' Bill would say tiredly. 'Try it again.'

This time I would slink on like a second-hand car salesman.

'I *wish* your enterprise today may thrive.'

'No, goddamn it, no! Where do you think you are – on a Sunday excursion to Niagara-on-the-Lake? Get some menace into it. This is great history, the fall of the mightiest Caesar. Can't you feel it?'

'Oh, I can feel it okay. I just can't say it.'

In the end I defeated Bill, just as I had Henry, and my performance as Popilius Lena was not fraught with subtle implication. It was just bad, but not noticeable. As a matter of fact, I've just consulted the text and find that I actually had two lines. The second was: '*Fare you well.*'

I never got my name in lights or in the papers, or almost never. I did at last receive two reviews, one good, one bad, and I'm proud of them equally because the good review, 'In the part of Discretion, Hugh Hood was passable,' was a mistake. My name appeared in the programme:

DISCRETION . . . . Hugh Hood

But I didn't actually appear in the production.

A chap I knew called Clement Goforth, an enthusiast of the sacral drama, a pillar of Saint Mike's Music and Drama Society, and like myself without acting talent, decided one day that the college should mount a production of the early sixteenth-century morality play of *Everyman.* Religious, you see, and allegorical as all hell, so he figured it was right for Saint Mike's.

A performance of this piece is hedged around with awful dangers. For one thing, it runs well over an hour in performance and is very hard to cut. For another, its action and language are by no means typical of the modern theatre, and except to antiquarians the play can only be in the last degree boring. And for one reason or another Clement could never get his cast together for rehearsals – some were in other shows, some were playing intramural hockey, some were goof-off types. I kept hearing about his troubles and when he asked me to play Discretion I discreetly refused. He stuck my name in the programme anyway, thinking I'd change my mind, and on the night of the performance doubled, or more accurately quadrupled, the part himself. He played four parts in all including that of God, the only one he'd originally planned to do.

No rehearsals, no cast – it was hell out there. When the lad who was to speak to Prologue came on, he literally had to be pushed from the shelter of the wings, cringing with fear. It was at once evident that he knew no lines whatsoever – the bookholder read each line for him, sometimes two or three times over, and he at length retired covered with mortification. Then the play began.

None of the actors knew any lines – except Clement, that is, and he knew them all. His voice could be heard all over the theatre, prompting, exhorting, and when he was onstage in any of his four roles he could be heard reading not only his own speeches, but those of everyone else. He delivered the lines which had been slated for me, Discretion, with fire and intelligence, and seemed quite carried out of himself by the sequence of events. In the fourth and greatest of his parts, that of the Deity, he appeared way up on top of an eight-foot level in a cotton-batting beard, with a flowing cape made from an old terrycloth beach robe. The effect was indescribable.

Kind, decent Nathan Cohen was sitting a few rows in front of me. His shoulders had been vibrating gently for several minutes prior to Clement's apotheosis, but when he epiphanized in this way it was too much for Nathan. He began to shake all over – I thought with outrage and resentment – and hurried up the aisle and out of the house. I followed him into the cloakroom and found him standing by a water-fountain, purple all right, but with laughter, not rage. He'd been afraid that he'd begin to shriek uncontrollably and embarrass the actors, and he'd just got out in time.

Next day in *The Varsity* I got my good review, and everybody else in the play caught hell. The reviewer started off pretty lively: 'Last night at Hart House the Saint Michael's College Music and Drama Society unveiled a revolutionary new concept of dramaturgy in which each line of dialogue is first spoken twice by an offstage voice and a third time by the visible actor.' He was very hard on Clement: 'Not content with perpetrating this abortion upon an unsuspecting and wholly innocent public, Clement Goforth had the audacity to come before us in the role of God!'

This same reviewer gave me my other mention when I played Lodovico in the Hart House *Othello*. Not at all a bad part, Lodovico, running to two scenes and maybe twenty lines, including the last speech of the play. Just before Othello kills himself, Lodovico rather nastily says to him:

... your power and your command are taken off
And Cassio rules in Cyprus.

I somehow got the idea that Lodovico, a Venetian emissary of exalted rank and powers, ought to be rendered in a strangulated English accent, a version of James Mason. And the only place I could find to establish this conception solidly was in my pronunciation of the word 'command,' which I insisted on delivering as if it rhymed with 'bond' or 'pond.' *Commond.*

The company begged me to abandon this phony English accent, and particularly on *commond,* but it got to have a hypnotic fascination for me and I'd get rid of it in one rehearsal only to come out with it in the next. The cast were on pins and needles every night as I approached the dreaded word; it was like driving a runaway team of horses. I'd be going peaceably along through my big ten-line speech and the other players would start to stare at me in fixed horror, and I just couldn't stop:

> ... *your power and your* (pause) COMMOND *are taken off*

It shook the audience badly and had a ruinous effect on the curtain. And *The Varsity* reviewer said: 'As Lodovico, Hugh Hood let the play down with a dull thud.' That was the end of my acting career as far as the press was concerned.

They never caught me when I was good, that's all. Once and only once I *was* good, quite by accident, in the Gill production of Rodney Ackland's dramatization of *Crime and Punishment* in which Gielgud had played Toronto the season before. This is a curious and perhaps finally unworkable play, a sprawling acting version of a sprawling novel, which really demands cinematic treatment because several actions have to be represented simultaneously, though supposedly in different places. Thus in the novel Raskolnikov lives in quite a different boarding-house from Sonia and Katerina Ivanovna; but in the play everybody in the cast, or pretty near, lives in the same house, in a complex one-set arrangement with little rooms all over the place. Katerina Ivanovna and her family occupy the downstage centre area, Raskolnikov lives in far right, almost in the wings. I and my slatternly wife, and a clerk who shares my quarters and presumably my wife, live in a little cupboard upstage centre behind Katerina Ivanovna. The three of us are onstage throughout the play, though we have only ten lines between us.

My slut of a wife was played by the beautiful Mary Waugh, and the villainous clerk by Dickie Butterfield of Trinity. We had a wonderful time all week inventing bits of business. Sometimes Mary would be lolling on my knee in the first scene, and on Dickie's in the second. Sometimes he and I would be quarrelling violently in pantomime. We were utterly relaxed and I lost that robot-like quality which normally marred my acting. In fact Henry Kaplan came to see the show and failed to notice that the loutish peasant lurking in the background throughout the piece was his old nemesis. I met him in Diana Sweets one night, and asked him how he'd liked the show.

'My God,' said Henry, 'are you in it?'

I told him who I was playing.

'Well, I don't understand that,' he said. 'I didn't recognize you at all.' He waved his hands expressively. 'Why, you were good!'

I even took a fairly prominent part in some of the downstage business, always as a sort of live prop. The play opens with Katerina Ivanovna, played by my old flame Betty Reilly, screaming at her children and beating them while she waits for the drunken Marmeladov to come home. At the curtain we get thirty seconds of din from Betty, and then I plead with her, from the door of my little room, to compose herself. She turns on me viciously and at this point the landlady, played by Clarine Jackman, comes rushing on to order Katerina Ivanovna to be silent or quit the boarding house. Katerina (Betty) rushes up to me and slaps my face, and tells the landlady to go to hell. I will say that old Betty had a solid right hand. Anyway this opener has to begin very very big and hold there for not more than half a minute, at which point the actual spoken dialogue begins.

On the final night of the run the Governor General, Lord Alexander, attended the show. You could easily spot him out front because he was in evening dress with miniatures, a ribbon and a star, and was surrounded by a retinue. Just before the curtain rose Bob Gill told us that he would be in the house and asked us to give our best performance to suit the occasion. This made Clarine a bit nervous because she suddenly disappeared somewhere, and wherever it was that she went, she got stuck. Somehow or other the door got wedged shut behind her, and there was no one nearby to answer her distracted thumpings and calls for release.

Up went the curtain. Betty launched into her tirade. Her children began to wail. I begged her to be silent. Thirty seconds had elapsed and suddenly there was a hush onstage. No Clarine. In the wings there was a great scurrying to and fro, and all at once we heard Bob's anguished whisper.

'Where's Clarine, for God's sake?' And then to us. 'Keep it up, kids, keep it up, do something, anything!'

Here my great moment began. Realizing that the entire beginning of the play was meant to be incoherent in any case, that in short anything was permitted, I launched myself forward from the door of my little upstage cubicle, to the astonishment of Mary and Dickie. I took the fullest and most impressive move downstage you ever saw, right down almost to the apron. I'd never been so prominent before, and though I moved as though I'd been hung from a trolley-wire, I felt completely master of the situation, a rare and heady sensation.

When I was level with Betty I made a precise right turn, crossed to where she was cowering on a trunk and glared sternly at her.

'Now look here, little mother, I mean to say,' I began at the top of my voice. I had just finished reading *The Brothers Karamazov* and threw in a few Constance Garnett versions of Dostoievsky. 'Only fancy, Katerina Ivanovna, my brother the shoemaker who lives in K. Street, my unfortunate brother with his wife and seven ragged children, with fifteen roubles a month to feed and clothe his family, enjoys more peace of mind in a miserable garret not half the size of this room, more innocent family joy, than a traveller might discover in fifty versts of galloping, and hard galloping at that. And why? I will tell you why. His house is a quiet house whereas here, my esteemed Katerina Ivanovna, one finds the most constant disorder. Ach, tfoo, it's a disgrace and all that.'

Betty stared at me as if bewitched and then all at once she collected her wits, leaped off the trunk and began to rummage inside it wildly, eventually producing some ragged pieces of children's clothing which she held up for my inspection.

'A disgrace is it, Pyotr Alexeievitch?' She made up the name on the spur of the moment. 'A disgrace you say? Why at this very moment my drunken cur of a husband is lying under a table in the gin-shop next his office. Yes, lying in a stupor, the beast, whilst I struggle to preserve a humble shelter over the heads of his children. I'm a colonel's daughter, a gentlewoman, Pyotr Alexeievitch, I'll have you to understand, and not a wretched kulak strayed in from the Orel district like yourself. How dare you address me in such a way!'

We carried on like this for about two minutes, enjoying ourselves hugely and even getting a few laughs, and at last Clarine burst irrationally onstage and the action of the play began, a little late. Nobody in the audience realized that anything had gone wrong. Some veteran playgoer might have wondered why a small-part actor should have such big speeches in the first scene and nothing to do thereafter; but nobody's evening was spoiled and we proceeded smoothly to the conclusion. That was the last play I was in. From first to last I was in twenty-five shows – I had their names inked on a shoebox in which I kept my makeup. I often wonder what became of that shoebox and I wish I had it now because it would make a nice souvenir.

Things theatrical began and ended for me with Betty Reilly, in my first important show and my last. Like so many of those good university actors and actresses she stayed in the professional theatre, in a number of summer-stock groups, in a brief whirl in New York, in television where she's very big, and very prominently these days at Stratford.

I've never been to Stratford, and now I don't suppose I ever will go. My wife worked there for quite a while and maybe one member of the family is enough in that connection. I've only seen Betty on television since she matured as an actress, and I guess as a woman too; she sure as hell isn't an ingenue now. She's a star, almost the only Toronto actress who has the real strong star quality. She bursts out of the little screen at you even in a bad play, with those huge eyes and the rowdy voice and the quality of inner hurt.

Maybe I should have kissed her that time on the sofa. I'm a happily married man, God knows, a state I wouldn't willingly change. But I sit there evenings, watching the TV screen, and when old Betty Reilly comes on I smile at my wife, and she smiles back. She knows! And I always wonder what it would have been like.

Educating Mary

WHEN A LOVED, admired, and respected nephew, a scant half generation younger than oneself, marries a lovely and docile young wife to whom one has introduced him, it is a carelessly self-absorbed uncle who pays no attention to the chain of events he has almost inadvertently set in motion. I am not a man who meddles in others' affairs – I believe that anyone who knows me will tell you that – and I would as soon have had nothing to do with the marriage of my nephew to my former secretary. But there it is; the situation is irretrievable, and one must make the best of it.

Ours is not a vastly ramified, loyal and affectionate family in the style of the nineteenth century and yet, when my nephew came down from Northampton upon his graduation from the law school, I felt obliged to smooth his path wherever possible. I am not greatly his senior, half a generation, fifteen years, if one must be brutal and state the precise cold figure; but I may perhaps have appeared to Francis something on the order of a sophisticate, a knowledgeable city-dweller. I took him, so to speak, under my wing, which sounds pompous and even stuffy, and is nevertheless true.

I didn't of course place him with his present legal connection; that was done as it is always done by an osmotic process that begins in school and is at length determined by one's choice of club. He had been destined for the bullpen at Willison, Besant, Dunlop and Nashe since his junior year. Nor did I find him an apartment, nor in any way try to censor his circle of acquaintance. His father is ten years my senior; we have never been as close as children in a less sporadic sequence of production might have been. I am one of a trio separated by five-year intervals, and my sister has been in some sense close to both her brothers, the nerve centre or cortex through which we have communicated. My brother and I are too disparate in age and interests to be much at ease with one another.

Francis resembles his father in very few respects but is very like his mother, to whom I was at one time much attached, and it may have been because of this attachment that I tacitly undertook to look after him in New York. To speak frankly, my brother is a lazy stuffed-shirt who conceals a do-nothing disposition under the title of manager of a family trust. Alice was much his superior and would have done more wisely to wait, as I entreated her to do, until I matured physically. As I was still in short pants when I communicated this plea, and as she was engaged to James at the time, my entreaties went ignored, or at least unacted-upon.

She would have done better to have married me, but that is water under the dam. Francis, her only child, resembles her physically in his colouring and general conformation. He is slight but strong, and has his mother's fine light-brown, almost blond, hair. I liked him at once, when he came down, and determined to do what I could to ease his way. I entertained him and passed much time in his company, and I introduced him to Mary Saunderson.

He was twenty-five, I should judge, and I forty, when we began to go about together as comrades, almost as men of the same generation. I have led a rather lonely life, I may as well admit, and I found Francis very good company. Neither of us was much accustomed to the society of women, and we made our lives out of the kind of thing such men do. We went shares in a Dragon for three seasons with some success in competition. We made a more than passable doubles team – I taught Francis what he knows about playing the net – and we played considerable golf, or at least we did until we discovered that we had in common the almost ungovernable Stewart temper, something at least that he didn't derive from his mother. When we met in matchplay we quarrelled all the way around the course, and as we were very evenly matched our mutual irritation was so extreme from time to time as almost to end the friendship.

I THINK the Stewart temper is hereditary, doubtless having something to do with the body chemistry and metabolic rate of its possessors. I am not ill-disposed towards my fellow men when I am alone. I contemplate their lot with pity, and almost with sympathy, and am ready with my chequebook for every worthy cause. But I cannot endure much personal contact. The obtuseness, propensity towards untruth, evil inclination of the will, and natural bestiality, which experience teaches me to perceive in myself and others, so saddens and inflames me that I have sometimes offered violence at the sight of a vicious or ignoble act, and I have suffered hellish shame at my incapacity to behave in accordance with the dictates of my conscience.

Francis is the same. In society he can be dourly agreeable, unlike myself, which is why I am a solitary. But this is only with some effort, and some composure inherited from his mother. At bottom like myself and my otiose brother, his father, and like our father and his father, Francis has a ferocious disposition and a broad stripe of hostile aggression.

It is not the blood but the blood pressure. In a century, when human physiology begins to be understood (for the present state of medical science is plainly that of the most abject and debased superstition) some pharmacological genius will evolve the proper prescription for men afflicted as I am with a tendency for the top of the head to fly off when something is unduly upsetting.

Ought I to describe this sensation? Not everyone knows it, I think, and those who do not should pity those who do. *Etouffé.* That would be the French word, stifled, a feeling as if the veins would burst from a swelling of the blood or from their own constriction. The nearly spastic contractions of the neck muscles, the tremblings. I don't want to get mad at people but I do all the time, mostly at foolishness, sometimes at vice. I shall die at fifty-eight or so from damage to the musculature of the heart, and there is not much to be done about this.

Francis is the same, and he can be a copper-bottomed ring-tailed son of a bitch if he gets mad at you. He would say the same about me. It was with his constitution in mind that I introduced him to my secretary.

Don't suppose that I'm going to tell you what business I am in, or that I mean to divulge any of my professional interests. They are those appropriate to a man of my station in life, age, and temperament, which is all that needs to be said. I have had a number of secretaries – how I obtain them is my own affair, but there is nothing criminal about it. My secretary must be three things, beautiful, intelligent, docile. I may say that I have had almost all of my secretaries married out from under me, to use a faintly indelicate turn of speech, and they have all married well except the last, who is about to. Of all this royal sisterhood, Mary Saunderson excited the most kindly feelings in my breast. I created her *ex nihilo,* as it were, endowed her with every female treasure, and at last married her to my nephew. Nowadays she would tell you a different story, but this is substantially what occurred.

WHEN MARY came to me in 1956 she was a dowdy child from the less fashionable part of upstate New York, not Saratoga, but a little town west of Hudson called Cobleskill with little to recommend it apart from some pleasing Federal architecture. She had attended a secretarial academy in her native town, and had passed four semesters at the branch of the state university of New York in Binghamton. When she arrived in the city she was twenty-one, utterly uncultivated and at the same time unspoiled. How I found her is my affair, but I think I may reveal that the meeting was connected with my patronage of a home for unwed business girls which is conducted by the Congregational Church. Mary was that rarity, a Congregationalist from New York State, but Cobleskill is not far distant from the Berkshires, and the circumstance is not the anomaly it appears.

She was friendless and alone, with her principles and her secretarial training to recommend her, and her appearance, and little more. Perhaps that is enough. The directress of the Crosby Home prudently recommended Mary to me. I engaged her on sight, her predecessor having informed me of her impending marriage some time before. This was a sly sharp girl, quite unlike Mary, who wore a near-grin as she announced her.

'A Miss Saunderson to see you, Mr Stewart.'

'That will do, Peggy.'

'Do?'

'You are leering. You had better go and attempt to put your files in order.' She laughed and withdrew, and Mary came around her and in the door. I shan't do justice to the bathos / pathos of her appearance, for I do not command the technical vocabulary of the *couturier*; but I know that she wore a straw boater with a ribbon down her neck, and that her masses of hair escaped in great coils down her back. I have rarely seen anyone who looked less what she purported to be. She carried a secretarial notebook under one arm, but I was not to be so easily taken in as that. Shorthand and typing are one thing, and tact and address another.

'You are Miss Saunderson?'

'Yes, sir.'

'And you wish employment as a secretary and stenographer?'

'Yes, sir.'

'And have you ever operated a telephone switchboard?'

'No, sir.'

I looked at her more closely – she had an oddly persuasive voice – and felt disposed to be kind. 'There are not many of us here and the switchboard is quite small, and uncomplicated, and you would not be at it all the time. Miss Wilenski could show you.'

'I think I could learn it, sir.'

'I am Mr Stewart.'

'Mr Stewart.'

I smiled at her; she was obviously a good girl, and so quiet. I hired her on the spot; she blushed and smiled and was all thanks. 'I am a foolish indulgent man,' I told her, 'and you will be overpaid, considering what you are able to do. But I expect that you will soon grow into your salary and after that, if you continue to improve, I shall increase it.'

'Thank you, sir.'

'Be sure to tell Miss Franklin that I inquired for her.'

'I will, I will.'

'But move out of the Crosby Home at once, otherwise it will infect you with parochialism.'

She looked at her skin in fright. 'What is that?'

I waved my arms as expressively as possible. 'You have been to a college, and don't know that word?' I spelled it.

'Oh,' she said, 'is that how you pronounce that?' She had seen the word, but no one had ever used it in her hearing.

'Find an apartment, and if the rents are beyond your means, let me know.'

She came into the office the next Monday and Peggy Wilenski took her in hand. Soon she was conversant with all, or almost all, of our affairs. She was not as penetrating or as slyly witty as Peggy, but was quite as intelligent in a more reflective way, and much better-looking, when once she had learned to exhibit herself to advantage, which took her about two years.

The first thing to go was her abundance of hair, which had so indicated her countrified origins. When she had been with us perhaps six months, she popped out of the elevator one morning with her head in a curious turban which she refused to take off. We all supposed at first that she had a cold in the head, as it was the middle of winter. As the office warmed her and the day drew on we expected her to remove her headdress, but she refused.

'I can't.' Sniffle.

'Are you in pain?'

'No, Mr Stewart.' More sniffling.

'Well, then, in the name of Almighty God, what is it?'

'Oh, I've done something foolish.'

'What?'

'I've had my hair cut. I don't know what my mother will say.'

'Let me see,' I said, actuated – I don't quite know why – by an extreme curiosity. She rose at once and retired, returning with surprising promptitude. Someone had administered what was known in those days as a 'feather cut' and though it is vulgar in me to say it, she looked 'cute,' there is no other word. She had certainly managed to choose a good hairdresser. 'Why, Mary,' I said, more to console her than anything, 'that looks most attractive, and more suitable to office work.'

She brightened up a good deal at this. 'Do you like it?'

'Why, yes, as you ask me.'

'Then it doesn't matter what my mother thinks.'

'It always matters what your mother thinks, my dear.'

'Yes, Mr Stewart.' Her little curls and feathers floated around her head very pleasingly.

The metamorphosis of Mary proceeded at a deliberate but steady pace. Her straw boater appeared once or twice during her second summer with us, but not thereafter, and after her initial haircut, unlike the biblical hero, she went from strength to strength. As I review this development I often wonder at whom that first feather cut was aimed, and I fear – I greatly fear –that it can have been directed at no one but myself.

It was with some faint intimations of this that I observed her emergence from the chrysalid state. I was at that time forty years old and had no formed intention of beginning a new mode of life in my fifth decade. I proposed to myself what I still propose, a solitary and meditative middle age succeeded by a comfortably early death from overstrain of the heart. I have no intention, nor had I then, of attempting either to shorten or to prolong my span of life by taking a wife. But I now see what I only glimpsed then by half-lights and shadows, that Miss Mary's studies in propriety were, if not actuated by interest, at least not motiveless.

I don't know that she apprehended this herself; but the fact is that each successive epiphany was communicated first to me. In the year when they were fashionable – was it 1958, how long ago it seems – she wore sack dresses of an unquestionably provocative character and yet, and yet, they could not be faulted on the grounds of immodesty unless the critic had himself a smack of coarseness. Her sack dresses were like herself, apparently innocent in what they hinted, but very likely calculated. As we know, the cut of such a frock is of a nature to appear loose and unfitted, but it will in fact catch and cling just here, just there, arbitrarily, or so it seems.

How can one tell the appearance from the fact? I had no wish – I have none now – that this young woman reveal the precise topography of her body to my astonished gaze. I once or twice remonstrated with her.

'My dear child,' for I was as yet unaware of the power of her will, 'my dear Mary, is not that dress, ah ... ah. Hmmmn.'

'Is there something wrong with it, Mr Stewart?'

'Are you quite comfortable in it?'

'Oh, yes, it's so nice and cool. No sleeves, you see.'

'I understand. But isn't it, in places, the merest shade ... tight?'

'Tight?'

'Well, yes, tight.'

The cunning thing grasped bunches of the dress material between her fingers in just those places where there was fabric to spare. 'Why, Mr Stewart,' she said ingenuously, 'it's loose, loose, see?' And she held the crushed material forward as far as possible. I bent my head and recommenced my dictation, and I will confess that I kept my head lowered for some time. When at length I raised it, I saw that Mary's face was suffused with a crimson blush, and though I said nothing out of the order of business I understood that she had taken my meaning. And yet she persisted in wearing such articles, I am sure because she knew that I had been, if anything, more out of countenance than she.

There were other matters. Her scent, though always discreet, was extraordinarily varied, and as her salary increased the variety and subtlety of these perfumes increased proportionately. New York is warm in the summertime, and the merest hint of scent will pervade the largest office and persist, supported no doubt by the humidity. One felt like a honeybee among fresh flowers.

I DETERMINED to marry her off instanter. I cast my eyes around and just here I erred. All unbeknownst to him, I concluded that the best thing for all of us would be for Mary to marry my nephew Francis. I liked the girl and enjoyed her appearance and her submissiveness. I was fond of Francis when we were not opponents on the links. I supposed that happy relations would subsist among the three of us, and I took the fatal step. I began to take Francis to lunches at the university club. He would come uptown, lounge for ten minutes next to Mary in the receptionist's quarters, then at length I would appear and we would go along. I always gave him time to establish, and later to develop, the friendly relationship which grew up between him and my secretary. I 'threw them together' and though Mary was now between sacks and shifts her beauty was sufficiently in evidence to penetrate Francis' consciousness.

Ostensibly oblivious to this burgeoning courtship, I played the part of kind, youngish uncle and confidant. I never discussed the young woman. I waited, and to do Mary justice I hadn't long to wait. We were dividing two dozen oysters one brisk afternoon in the first of the months with an 'r' when Francis raised his eyes from his plate and began to speak of Mary.

'That's a very fine-looking girl, that Miss Hoo-Haw.'

I swallowed an oyster and drank the juice and said nothing.

'You know who I mean?'

I rolled an earnest eye at him. 'According to Freud, jokes on personal names are signs of deep hostility. What is the person's name?'

'Miss Saunderson.'

'Ah.' The waiter came with butter. 'Ahhhhh.'

'Your secretary.'

'What about her?'

He looked wildly at his oyster. 'I am in love. I love her, oh, I love her. She is everything to me.' He may not have used precisely this diction, but it captures his tone.

'My dear Francis ...'

'Have I your permission to pursue the matter?'

'Pursue what matter?'

'I wish to make her my wife.' That is what he should have said, but my nephew, in the vulgar idiom of the modern young said only, 'I wanna give her a go-round.'

I made some token objections which went unheard.

'I love her to distraction ...' and much more to the same effect, some of which I thought overstated, and some in questionable taste. But I allowed myself to be talked around, and when we returned to the office, I had in effect bartered off my secretary in exchange for my peace of mind. It was settled that Francis might continue to court her in the reception room while he was waiting for me, but that he would not otherwise take up her time during office hours, with flowers and importunate telephone calls. What she did at night was naturally her own affair. I am not naïve enough to believe that the courtship was carried forward wholly in our reception room, and so imagine that Francis saw considerable of Mary between the opening of the oyster season and Christmas, when their engagement was announced.

I had looked for a certain amount of obloquy from Northampton on account of my ambiguous part in the affair, but there came none. It seems that Francis had trundled his darling home with him on a series of glorious autumn weekends. She had captivated his mama, my dear Alice, and so they were married and did not live happily ever after. Francis had, as I have noted, the violent Stewart temper, and his instinct in every domestic disagreement was to go at once for the jugular; early in their life together he began to say things to Mary that she could not believe he'd said, as she thought them over later. To these unspeakable accusations he communicated a tolerable amount of wristy follow-through.

'Stupid bitch!' I can hear my own accents, and his father's, and our father's, in Francis' expostulatory tone.

'Boo hoo.' We have all seen female tears rendered so, in the comic papers, but Mary's reproachful sobs actually sounded like that. When she wept, she said, 'Boo hoo,' the only woman I've ever known who did so. It used to drive Francis wild. I remember the first time they asked me to dinner after their union, when they were still living on 87th Street near Second Avenue, before they began to feel too close to Harlem. I arrived about eight o'clock and was happily seated in their infinitesimal drawing room holding a glass of sherry when Francis entered, nibbling an olive.

'Cleanses the palate,' he said and then he noticed my glass. 'What's that?'

'A glass of sherry.'

'Who gave you that?'

'Mary, who else?' It took the remainder of the evening for us to get him down from the ceiling. He stamped into the kitchen, or as far in as he could get. There was scarcely room for two in that kitchen, as I remember it, and the entire apartment, advertised as four and a half rooms, was in fact no bigger than a moderately spacious hotel room, which may have given Francis claustrophobic feelings, intensifying his customary ill-humour.

'Sherry,' he roared at his defenceless wife, 'who taught you to give a guest a fortified wine before dinner? An almond perhaps, or possibly an olive. But sherry? Where were you brought up?'

I made some deprecatory remarks which he took extremely ill.

'I invite you particularly to sample a Graves and a Beaujolais. I expect you to be on the *qui vive,* and you drink sherry. You're as bad as she, *corruptio optimi pessima.*'

'You don't propose those as great wines, and if you did, would it be worth this fuss?'

'It's a question of principle, of the right conduct of life.'

'Principle doesn't excuse rudeness, Francis. I'm your guest, and I expect to be treated with courteous hospitality, and spared the witness of an ugly scene between husband and wife.'

'Ah, you old hypocrite,' he brought out in strangled tones. 'In my place you'd do just the same.' I must concede he had me there, because if a woman had transgressed in some matter which I took seriously, I too would have approached her with hostility and mistreatment. We shared the psychology of the old bachelor, and I guess it is an odious one, nine parts selfishness and one part sloth. It is not with entire injustice that housewives believe that all bachelors urinate as a matter of course in washbasins and kitchen sinks, or whatever other vessel is at hand.

I had drawn Francis' fire, and he spent the evening plying me with recondite information about viniculture, some of which he had without doubt mugged up out of some book or other. I have never quite grasped what he was getting at that first evening, whether he was asserting an unshared dominion over his spouse, or perhaps making it clear that she was in his service now, and not mine. He played to the hilt the role of master *chez lui,* and the spectacle furnished me with much food for reflection.

His wife watched us with round hurt eyes; but she did not lose control of herself, nor did she spoil the meal as a more easily flustered young woman might have done. Francis had attacked her almost with brutality, had made her cry in front of an old acquaintance, had thoroughly mastered her, as it appeared, and yet her biscuits were good and hot and the meat not overdone. The bite of the sherry had gone by the time my opinion was solicited in the matter of Francis' Graves.

'Can you really taste it?' he demanded enthusiastically. 'I should have thought she'd ruined your judgement for the evening.'

'Not at all. I drank very little sherry.'

'What do you think of this?'

I never know what to say about wine but I never let on, and so pass as an authority. 'It tastes a little straw-coloured,' I said decisively.

'Exactly,' said Francis.

'But the after-bouquet lies well in the nasal passages and throat.'

'My opinion to a T.'

Mary looked from one of us to the other without a word, but with perhaps the hint of a smile, paying close attention. That was scarcely five years ago, and today she passes for the smartest of young married *Société Escoffier* hostesses, whose wine service is unexcelled.

SHE LEARNED nothing instantly and she took many cruelly wounding blows whilst Francis was bringing her up to his standard of sophistication. It strikes me now, though it didn't then, that he might have guessed that while he taught her wine and food service, and net-play, and parlour psychoanalysis, he was inadvertently teaching her something else; but this never crossed his mind, nor mine.

There is a kind of inverse proportionality operating in any such relationship; the more one indulges his ill temper as a whip with which to discipline his partner, the less the sting is felt. The dog will chase the mechanical rabbit almost endlessly, but at last even he, poor fool, will sit on his haunches and loll out his tongue. Any coercive stimulus of that sort will lose its force as its object becomes inured to it. Francis growled and griped and carried on, and at first Mary wept, and then held back her tears, and then awoke to the lessening of the smart. I saw her once at the halfway mark, when Francis asked her to crew for him one Saturday.

'No,' she said, with downright good humour, 'I don't believe that I will.'

'What do you mean, you won't?'

'What anyone means.'

He was silent for some moments and then said, 'Why not?'

'Because I don't enjoy it. I don't want to drive halfway out Long Island before breakfast and fry in ninety degrees of sunshine and be wet through as well and miserable for eight hours, and exhausted at the end.'

'But damn it, I like it.'

'Then you go,' she said, and wouldn't be budged.

After that, certainly, he might have seen the end. Having grasped that her independence lay in vigorous self-assertion and a loud voice and a deliberately hurtful vocabulary, Mary grew experimental. She began to test out how far she could go, initially with little denials, and refusals such as I have illustrated, then with progressively more grave declarations, to which it was vain of her husband to reply with threatened violence; she had grown as violent as he.

They stood face to face in the kitchen and glared at each other. 'I ought to slap your silly face.'

'If you lay a hand on me, I'll call the police.'

This could not be ignored, so he hit her, and though she did not call the police her riposte was quite as effective. She picked up a kitchen chair, lifted it over her head, and smashed it down on the edge of the sink, shattering it. Then she did the same with a second. They were old and cheap chairs which they had re-finished together, and most likely the glue had dried and the wood grown brittle, but the strength and violence of the act amazed and repelled Francis. Mary ran out of the apartment and did not return for several hours; she proffered no explanation on her absence and he didn't care to demand one.

An uneasy balance obtained for eighteen months, while their mutual capacity for violence and outrage was on a level. At length, however, Francis began to feel not precisely defeated but tired with the whole comedy, which had come to seem stale and repetitive.

'I'm bad-tempered,' he would protest, 'but not so much as to misbehave all the time; it's exhausting.' He began to wish that he had concealed the power of his passions, the accuracy and sting of his modes of attack, and the aphrodisiac effect upon him of their quarrels. He had taught her too much and too well.

'I'm not convinced that she means all of it,' he kept repeating. 'I suspect she's simply showing off her training. It makes me laugh. She used to weep silently when I abused her; now she grows violent and abusive. It's hard to tell which is worse.'

'Mary violent and abusive?'

'Like a fishwife. You wouldn't believe it unless you saw it. That's what's so galling, nobody believes it. You don't believe it. Everyone fancies I'm a monster and that butter wouldn't melt in her mouth. It's wonderfully distressing.'

'I'm amazed,' I said. 'I wish I could see her in action.'

'Come,' said Francis, 'you can't reasonably expect me to incite my wife to riot just to show her off. Besides, she's crafty. In front of you she'll be all sweet, reluctant, amorous delay, all for God in me, if you follow me.'

'Yes, I see. I can't spy on you.'

'No one feels the weight of it,' he said morosely, 'but me.'

As things fell out, he was wrong. I was to have the chance to observe the fully matured Mary in flood, or nearly so, and this quite accidentally. We had gone to Lincoln Center *à trois* to see Paul Schofield, a favourite of mine, who had been wholly inaudible, though exquisite indeed to behold. On our way across town afterwards, Mary was peppery, not to say shrewish, and yet I was certain that she was role-playing, as we say nowadays.

'Fools to design that stage so,' she expostulated. 'It's a second fiasco. I believe the entire project's doomed to ignominy and desuetude.'

'Ignominy and desuetude,' thought I to myself. Who can have taught her that diction? She cast a melting eye upon me.

'Francis, the boob, never took it into his head to ask about our seats. Simply chucks forty-five dollars down the drain.'

'You're being unjust,' said Francis stoutly. He was never intimidated by her, remaining a doughty antagonist till the end. 'I was entitled to assume that seating at that price would enable us to hear.'

'Not at Lincoln Center,' she said. 'For there we can take nothing for granted but fumbling mismanagement.' She dilated upon the follies of the promoters of this great public undertaking; the quarrel began to acquire intensity. Thinking it better to leave them, I motioned to our driver to stop.

'Not going?' asked Mary maliciously. 'We're just rounding into form.'

'Thanks. I believe I'll walk from here, for the fresh air.'

They drove away and I could hear her exclaiming. 'Screw you, Francis Stewart,' as they went. I was alarmed and dismayed, and with good reason.

The divorce proceedings are moving apace, and this rapacious girl will be loosed upon an unsuspecting community not long hence. I am not sure that I can face this prospect with a decent equanimity, inasmuch as my situation promises to grow very serious at her return. I have been meditating on her language 'ignominy and desuetude' and similar phrases, 'self-corrupting rapacity,' 'deluded obtuseness,' trouble me obscurely. Why should her eye melt as it rests on me? And yet it does, or did, and that not long since. And I have had these letters bearing the incredible salutation, 'My darling Charles.' Who gave her leave to address me by my Christian name, and as her darling? I am forty-nine, with but a decade to go by my reckoning, and without the energy to undertake any person's re-education, without the inclination to be myself reformed.

'My darling Charles.' Hmmmn.

I should be calm and consider. I should keep my head on my shoulders and my wits about me. I must keep my head. I must!

The Granite Club

I MET HER at the Granite Club during the luncheon for the start of the campaign. I'd only been on the women's committee three months, and hadn't met either of them before. You don't get on the women's committee till you're over thirty – should I admit that? When you're younger, you work for the Junior League or Hadassah or ... I don't know what the ethnic group wives do; they likely don't have the money. You don't come along and join the Society, you get asked *if* you have the money, *when* they decide they want you. I worked for Jewish General, for Beth Tzedec, Green Areas for Our Youngsters, I avoided the other organized charities. I wanted the Society from the start, a good product – we won't be out of business for a while, as Dan would have said.

It was Dan Slattery this, and Dan Slattery that, when I went there, something I wondered about because he was a professional and you know what they're like. Claim they can do better for you than you can manage on your own, and they're right. They have the lists and the Addressograph plates, the statistics, experience in other cities. They treat you like amateurs and you know they wish you stupid ladies would get out of the charity business and leave it to them or the government. I don't like them.

Distinguished citizens of our community don't like them either. Who likes to be used, to be a figurehead?

Mr Larkin Melady,
Chairman, Business and Industrial Wing.
Mr Samuel Grosskurth,
Chairman, Institutional Giving.
Mr Justice M.R.A. Bondholder,
Chairman, Government Liaison.
Mrs R. Arthur Diplock,
Chairman, Women's Committee.

Seen opening the clinic reading from left to right. Three

columns. I meant to be head of the women's committee when the time came. Mrs Lazarus Ciglen, chairman, women's committee. You have to work up. And at that I had a sub-committee of my own, bandages and dressings, before I'd been with them three months. I got good experience at the General, and with Laz for a husband I would know how to buy. Twice he got me absorbent cotton at a price, another time it was elastic tape, I was good on that sub-committee from the start, about the time I met them. Her. At the Granite Club.

It made us all mad that he wasn't there for our luncheon; he'd been at the men's the day before. Then he flew to Winnipeg and passed us up, which I thought a bad move for an employee. You have to keep in with the girls, not send your wife.

That plum carpeting! It wasn't too long ago I wouldn't have been allowed in and I didn't see even a token Negro, the one you rent for the occasion. What the carpet does to a dress you shouldn't see. Not plum, deep maroon, like rare beef under fluorescent light. And chiffon, shantung, crepe on a lot of the old girls, can you see it? I wore black wool and good costume jewellery, and Mrs Slattery came along looking a bit frightened in a flowered blue silk with some red in it, with a little jacket, smoothing her hair which always floated out in thin strands. I have thick black hair myself, and lots of it, all over.

She was peeking at the place-cards. I had her spotted and it couldn't be anybody else, from the dress and her hair.

'Aren't you perhaps Mrs Slattery?'

'Oh, I am, I was looking ... It's a big affair. My husband ...'

I thought, what's so great about Slattery, with somebody like this?

'You're at the head table, Mrs Slattery, would you like to come with me? I wonder if you've already met Mrs Diplock, this year's ...'

'I know Mrs Diplock to see her. Isn't she nice?'

'Very nice.'

Funny thing, she was nice, in that way that places you. Wearing navy, no make-up, smoothly brushed brown hair, nice. She gave me a big smile and took Mrs Slattery off my hands. When she called on the little woman for a few words, later on, it was a toss-up whether she'd get through it. She looked like a peahen, short, not exactly plump, without any specific kind of body, dry skin, that dress, and a lot of nervous mannerisms.

'SOMEBODY NAMED Mandy Ciglen. Mandy!'

'You didn't enjoy yourself?'

'I don't know what your father had in mind. I can't speak. Ever since I had elocution with Miss Patterson in my entrance year, I've been nervous about public speaking. Besides I don't work for the Society and I don't know anything about it.'

'What did you say?'

'Happy I am to be here ... sharing my husband's enthusiasm ... the maimed, the halt and the blind ... best kind of community co-operation ... have to keep charity personal ... Dan not a professional in his own mind, thinks of it as an honorarium ... which it is.'

'You don't say that though.'

'When people talk about an honorarium, they mean the money isn't enough. Your father is in a difficult position. Could you ask disease for a raise?'

Sally laughed and blew smoke. 'Sure.'

'Your father can't. He should have stayed in advertising.'

'I don't know, mother. Advertising is small potatoes outside of New York, even here. I don't think Dad wanted to stay there the rest of his life and besides, the pace is killing.'

'This is more my kind of place,' said Mrs Slattery, looking around Simpson's Arcadian Court, a graceful room in English Palladian with much light. 'I wouldn't want to belong to the Granite.'

'You needn't worry. It costs a lot.'

'I know it does. All those rich women working for love. Mandy Whatshername.'

A WEEK LATER Mrs Diplock came into the new clinic where we were all working away like little beavers, rolling and folding and pinning, with this utter charmer on her arm, a thin fellow, early fifties but marvellous-looking with that kind of hair that's mostly silver-grey but with plenty of black in it, very well-brushed, neat moustache. Energetic-looking. Men my own age are pushovers and you get tired of that, don't you? There was plenty of chirping and fluttering from the ladies' auxiliary. Then Mrs Diplock called me over.

'I don't think you've met Mr Slattery yet, dear. Dan, this is Mandy.'

'Mandy who?' he said, laughing a lot for some reason.

'Mandy Ciglen, Mrs Lazarus Ciglen. She's only been with us a few weeks. She's a darling.'

I said, 'I am not a darling, I'm a wild, wicked woman. It's well known.'

Mrs Diplock smiled vaguely and went over to talk to Daisy Lemmon, nose-swabs and Elastoplast, and this Slattery fellow gave me quite a careful scrutiny. Not sexy, more appraising.

'What do you think of the work we're doing?'

'Why,' I said, 'since you ask me, I think it's too amateur, which isn't a bad thing as long as it isn't something a lot of nice girls do, when they can get down from Forest Hill two hours a week. The way to lick this thing, if there is a way which I doubt because the death rate is always going to be one hundred percent, disease or no disease, but if there is a way, it's got to come from very expensive research running to hundreds of millions of dollars, and when you remember that the entire objective of our annual campaign doesn't exceed five million ... I'm running out of breath.'

'Breathless women are attractive,' he said, and ran his fingers through his hair. 'It's a question how long privately organized charities will continue to exist. When they go, I'll be a superfluous man, which is why I think about it. And then of course I'm taking money when I ought to work for nothing.'

That was always on his mind.

'Rabbis and priests take money.'

'Priests don't ask for raises.'

'They do so. Why, there's even talk of a priests' union. A man of God is entitled to the best salary he can bargain for.'

'I never thought of that. Perhaps I'm being too conscientious ... But don't tell Mrs Diplock I'm going to ask for a raise.'

'But you aren't, are you?'

'No. They vote me an increase at the annual meeting, generous, but never open to criticism, I oughtn't to complain.'

He waved at Mrs Diplock as she passed out of the room, and asked if I'd had lunch. 'I've got to eat quick, and go and see an airplane manufacturer,' he said.

'I haven't eaten,' I said, 'and you must mean Paul Sampson, the young one.'

'The young who?'

'The young Sampson. Not his father, I mean. I know Paul fairly well, and who else makes airplanes around here?'

'We'll have lunch together, then, and you can tell me about him. We want him on the board this year, and perhaps as chairman next year; airplanes are good publicity. And he's young. Not a bad thing, that.'

'I'm glad you approve.'

'Oh, you're not young. You're a natural force.'

He took me to a place called Csardas where they featured a very good goulash with a wine sauce; neither an expensive place nor a joint, a tactful selection. I found out afterwards that he never charged a meal to the Society except when he was travelling, and even then he wouldn't charge his lunch, only the meals he'd normally have at home.

'Yes. Well, Paul is attractive, not just an inheritor. He's gotten orders his father wouldn't have got, built the company up. His father is mainly a designer, very good too.'

'You seem to know a lot about them.'

'As I say, Paul is cute. Wrong word. He has a lot of chutzpah.'

'People like that flock together.'

'I suppose you keep yours hidden?'

'I have none.'

He always mentioned himself in the briefest terms. He would say nothing about his personal life, his wife for example, beyond what politeness required – the formal acknowledgement that he was married, had grown children, a home to go to. He never seemed to be aware of his attractiveness to women. Sometimes, I remember, towards the end of the campaign, after a late-afternoon conference, he would start to look his age. Then there was something sad about him.

'I DON'T KNOW why they fuss over him like that.'

'Dad has a lot of personality.'

'That's such a silly word, Sally.'

'Silly Sally. I don't think it's silly. I don't think you pay enough attention to him.'

'My own husband? We've been married over thirty years.'

'I guess he has emotions like anybody, or do people your age stop?'

'They stop having foolish emotions. Your father is no Clark Gable, you know.'

'Then you've nothing to worry about.'

'I don't see why they fuss over him. I don't. He wouldn't like it.'

'How do you know?'

THE YEAR Paul Sampson served on the board, just before he got to be chairman, I began to be a kind of special favourite of Dan's. He took me off bandages and dressings and gave me a lot of responsibility, so much that I hardly ever got home to my husband. I might just as well have been a full-time paid employee. Laz used to needle me about it; he didn't care; Laz has no feelings to speak of.

'Sweetie, you're marvellous, you're a dynamo.'

'I'm a natural force.'

'I'll see you when I get back from Cleveland.'

'Good trip, Laz.'

'Always a good trip, baby.'

Dan began to take me on field trips, with slides and film-strips and campaign posters and literature. We'd drive to one of the smaller cities, be present at a luncheon. Sometimes he spoke, sometimes I did. I got so I could give a pretty good talk on the costs of research from the woman's point of view. There's a woman's point of view on everything, it seems: LSD, foreign affairs, fiscal policy, the population explosion, you name it.

I have never been a one for the back country, but I loved those trips. One of the few situations where a man and a woman can show up together, with their respective spouses (spice?) lurking in the background, without prejudice to anybody's reputation. We went around together under the protection of sweet charity; who could fault that? And all that time I never got so much as a pat on my bottom from Dan, and I warn you, I'm no dog. I sometimes wondered what was the matter with him.

I guess I'm nothing but a trouble-maker. I'd have liked him to show a little affection that way, but he was a no-nonsense type, and they're the worst. You should have heard him give me hell over the Sampson business; you'd have thought it was all my fault. He knew Laz. He knew what Laz was. What Laz and I had for each other was amused toleration, great, but cooling to sleep with. We got married because we were expected to; it worked out beautifully and united two investment portfolios, and he is one of my oldest friends. He may screw all over Cleveland and Buffalo, no doubt he does, but you can't prove it by me, and anyway I don't care. I know I'm not making myself clear. I *like* Laz.

I never figured on a big stink about Paul. I certainly had no intention of bringing his emotional problems to the boil. I've never even met his wife. From all I hear she's a washed-out little piece, a doer of good works. I batted an eye. One eye; one bat. And he was turned on, and it was off to the races, you never saw anything like it. I mean, I don't see how I could have known. I was just nice to him because he said he'd make me chairman of the women's committee.

He started interrupting schedules Dan and I had worked out, and insisted on making what he called personal appearances, on our field trips. He used to go over very big with the audiences at out-of-town lunches, and if it was pats on the bottom I wanted, I could always count on a couple from Paul. At first the cursory chummy kind, later on the lingering ones, and then he started sneaking me away into corners while Dan was talking to local officials, and telling me that Betty was all wrapped up in the Hunt Club, which always used to make me howl with laughter.

'DAN, you're working too hard.'

'Yes, dear.'

'You know what the doctor said.'

'I do. I do.'

'Dan?'

'Hmmmn?'

'Are you all right?'

'A little tired tonight, nothing serious.'

'Dan, what's she like?'

'She's got a lot of energy, dear. She's a lot younger than we are.'

'Dan, I wish I could do something.'

'It's all right. I think you're fine the way you are. Anyway, it's too late to change.'

TWO DIVORCES, like winning the daily double, except that you get a bad name. But what could I do? Paul kept after me and Laz just laughed and laughed. God, it made me mad the way he treated me, and in the end I was on the point of saying the hell with it, and taking Paul on, just to see. I even thought of joining the Hunt Club, if you can imagine, but I don't suppose they'd have let me in, on account of having screwed Betty Sampson. Me on a horse!

Naturally there was dirty talk behind my back and I got kind of hung up over it, and wasn't sure what to do. I needed help. One Friday night in early October, just before the campaign opened, I was down at the office going over mailing lists and revising them out of the city directory, when Dan came in. He must have been working twelve to fourteen hours a day, never got home.

He said quietly, 'Why don't you knock it off, Mandy?'

'These have to be addressed in the morning.'

'They could wait, I said, why don't you knock it off?'

'How do you mean?'

'You know what I mean. You're only making mischief, aren't you?'

'What do you know about it? You don't know anything about it at all. You don't know my husband. Have you any idea what it's like to be a piece of furniture? Laz is a friend, he doesn't talk behind your back, but to him I'm nothing but home-furnishings, just something sitting on one side of the breakfast room around eight forty-five.'

'How did he get like that?'

'We had a good time in our twenties, when we were first married, and for a while afterwards. He took me on trips. Now all he cares about is the trade, and I don't know why.'

'When that happens nobody's to blame ... Or both are. I don't know which.'

'So I'm responsible?'

'I'm afraid so, and it would be the same with Paul; you'd find it out in three months.' He stopped talking and wandered around the office for a minute.

He had his back to me when I felt it, you know, and I kept quiet for once in my life, hoping he'd do something.

After a while he said, 'Mandy?'

'Yes, dear?'

'Uh-uh.'

I said, 'That peahen. That fool of a woman.'

'She's a little hysterical,' he said. 'That's all. At first I thought it was the menopause, but now I see it's always been this way.'

'Then leave her or something. Try me.'

'No. No. You stay with Laz. I couldn't do it, I don't know why. If she's always been this way, since she was younger than you are, I'm responsible.'

'Try Mandy's Instant Remedy. Heals all bruises.'

He wasn't listening. 'It's me,' he said. Despite his charm and energy, there was a break in him somewhere. He shook his head and said. 'It's Friday night, isn't it? Friday nights I go home to my wife. Don't worry about that mailing; it won't get there till Monday anyway.'

After he'd gone I sat in the office for a while, and then I got sick of what I was doing and went to wait for Laz. I think that was the second-last time I saw Dan.

AFTERWARDS Mrs Slattery said out loud, as if talking to Sally, though Sally wasn't there, 'You know, right till the very end, your father wanted to ... to. Usually on Friday nights. I always thought he was being silly.'

Checklist

1 'The Isolation Booth' was written in Hartford, Conn., in March 1957 and appeared in *The Tamarack Review,* No. 9 (Autumn 1958), pp. 5-12.

2 'The Perfect Night' was written in Hartford, Conn. in September 1957, and appeared in *Story,* 36, No. 4 (July-August 1963), pp. 101-107.

3 'The Winner' was written in Hartford, Conn., in October 1958, and appeared in *Jubilee* No. 3 (Spring 1976), pp. 4-21.

4 'The Fable of the Ant and the Grasshopper' was written in Hartford, Conn., in January 1959, and appeared in *Yes,* No. 13 (December, 1964), n.p.

5 'I'm Not Desperate!' was written in Hartford, Conn. in January, 1960, and appeared in *Exchange* 1, No. 1 (November, 1961), pp. 64-66.

6 'Friends and Relations' was written in Hartford, Conn., in June, 1960, and appeared in *Seven Persons Repository,* No. 6 (Spring 1973), pp. 1-9.

7 'The Changeling' was written in Hartford, Conn., in December, 1960, and appeared in *The Canadian Forum,* 41 (March, 1962), pp. 274-280.

8 'A Season of Calm Weather' was written in Hartford, Conn., in January, 1961, and appeared in *Queen's Quarterly,* 70 (Spring, 1963), pp. 76-93.

9 'Suites and Single Rooms, with Bath' was written in Montréal, in November, 1961, and appeared in '*Queen's Quarterly,* 79 (Autumn, 1972), pp. 366-373.

10 'The Ingenue I Should Have Kissed, but Didn't' was written in April, 1962, and appeared in *The Tamarack Review,* No. 25 (Autumn 1962), pp. 3-17.

11 'Educating Mary' was written in Montréal, in July, 1964, and appeared in *The Montrealer,* September, 1965, pp. 24-31.

12 'The Granite Club' was written in Montréal, in October, 1966, and appeared in *The Journal of Canadian Fiction,* No. 1 (Winter 1972), pp. 10-14.